Trouble In San Juan County

A western novel
By
ALEX ALEXANDER

LIFE IS JUST THE BLINK OF AN EYE
ETERNITY IS FOREVER

THIS NOVEL IS A WORK OF FICTION. ALL CHARACTERS AND EVENTS PORTRAYED IN THIS BOOK HAVE BEEN CREATED BY THE AUTHOR'S IMAGINATION AND REFER TO NO PERSON LIVING OR DECEASED.

TROUBLE IN SAN JUAN COUNTY
SECOND PUBLICATION

ALL RIGHTS RESERVED
Copyright © 2011 Alex Alexander

All rights reserved.

ISBN-10:1466413190
ISBN-13:9781466413191

DEDICATION

TO MY WIFE WHO HAS PUT UP WITH ME FOR SIXTY YEARS

Cover Art
By
Suzie Q.
and
Her Riders

Alex Alexander

Chapter One

Carlen Ashton dismounted from his line back dun horse at the top of the ridge and let his eyes wander through the streets of the bustling town. The main street was filled with all types of wheeled modes of transportation. There were wagons, buggies and buckboards along with every tie rail lined with saddle horses. He figured it was a trial or a hanging going on with this many people on the plank walks or crossing the street.

It was a fair size town compared to most of the ones he had passed through in the last two months. There was a strong river at the bottom of the ridge that curved to make its way about a hundred yards to run parallel to the main street. South of the river was the residential part of town where two wooden bridges spanned the river for the traffic to cross on. Giant cottonwood trees lined the river banks on each side. About a half a mile to the north of town was a tall bluff that ran for miles in an east west line. Above the bluff in the far distance he could see the snow capped peaks of the southern Rocky Mountains.

Carlen figured as many people that were in this area he could find a ranch that was hiring cowhands. He had killed a man in a fair gun fight that was forced on him three months ago in Alice, Texas. The man's friends and family were threatening to kill him regardless of what the law said was a fair fight. Witnesses testified that the man started the fight and pulled his weapon first. Carlen thought that to have to kill one man was enough. He told himself that if he left town they would call him a coward, but that was their problem. He wasn't afraid of any of them; he just didn't want to have to kill a bunch of revenge getters to prove that he wasn't a coward. He knew that he couldn't get a room for the night as crowded as the town was so he mounted his horse and rode through the heavily forested ridge to the north to find a good campsite for the night at the base of the bluff. He rode for a quarter mile and dropped from the ridge into a small grass filled meadow with a spring flowing toward the river. There was plenty of cover and grass for his mount. Why look any farther? Early the next morning he saddled his mount and headed toward town. He thought it was time for a sit down in a chair meal at a café. The last few days he had enough of his own cooking. The streets were deserted and it looked like a ghost town compared to the scene he watched late the day before. Well, at least there was a light showing in the windows of the huge general store. Painted in red letters on the hanging sign above the plank walk read, San Juan General Emporium. Carlen tried the front door and found it open, the bell above the door tinkled. An older bald headed man with rimless glasses hanging on his nose rose from behind the counter and said, "Good morning young man. May I help you with something?"

"Yes, Sir. I just rode into town and saw that you were the only place open, so I thought that you might tell me of a good place to have breakfast."

"Well I guess that because of the large crowd we had here until late last night the rest of the store owners are still in bed. I just got here myself and was fixing to start restocking. I sold a lot of merchandise yesterday and need to clean out my storeroom to see if I can replenish my empty shelves. The only cafe in town is usually opened before good daylight and is really a good clean place to eat."

"Well I guess I should mosey on down there and be their first customer."

"Young man I can tell that you are a Texan. I bet you haven't been in this country very long."

"Just to tell you the truth, I am a Texan, and a lost one at that. I really don't know where I'm at, New Mexico Territory or Southern Colorado."

The store owner gave him a smile and told him if he was on the south side of the river he was in New Mexico. If he was on the north side he was in Colorado. The older man walked from behind the counter and stuck out his hand and said, "I'm Farris Baker. A transplanted Texan myself." Carlen shook his hand and introduced himself.

"Carlen, I moved up here ten years ago from Central Texas to escape the summer heat. It was the best move of my life. The winters are longer here, but the air is not as damp and the cold is not as bad on me as it was in Texas. Maybe you will find a place to settle down."

"I would like to if I can find a good paying steady job. I figured that as many people as I have watched in town from the east ridge last evening that there must be a few large ranches around that might need a good cowhand."

"Well there is, but if you want a good paying job in town we are in need of a sheriff. The last one was killed by a gang of rustlers that ran off a bunch of cattle from old man Johnson's place. He has a large ranch that is located on the bench that is on top of the bluff north of town. The sheriff took a posse after the gang. They laid an ambush for them and wounded two men and killed the sheriff. That was six months ago and the town has not found a replacement yet. If you're interested I can get the town council to talk with you."

"To tell you the truth, Mister Baker, the reason I'm here was because in Texas I was a deputy and was forced to kill a man. I worked for the sheriff of Alice, Texas for five years and thought I could be an officer of the law without a killing. The man I killed was trying to kill me because I had arrested him twice. The man was a bad gambler and would call everyone he played with a cheater when he lost. He made the mistake of shooting one of the town's leading citizens and when I went to arrest him in the saloon he pulled on me and I was forced to shoot him. He has a few kinfolks that sought revenge, so before killing a few more I thought it best to let them cool off a while."

"Sure, I can understand your reason, but there is going to have to be a lot of the people killed that are on the wrong side of the law before this nation is settled. I can't understand why a man would hurt someone else and take from him what he has worked for all of his life. These kinds of ruffians are going to have to be jailed or killed before we have any peace in the west. Carlen, you think about the office of sheriff and if you would take the position we in San Juan would back you to the hilt."

"I'll give it some thought, Mister Baker. May I ask you why there were so many people in town yesterday?"

"Well, there were two reasons. One was that there was a Friday night social and dance at the Masonic Lodge and a discussion about the bank robbery we had a week ago. Someone broke into the town's only bank and cleaned it out. All of the folks around are up in arms because they thought their money was safe."

"You folks here sure are having a bad time with rustlers and robbers. I thought the Federal Government would insure the people's deposits."

"The banker never bothered to get the proper papers to the banking commission. All of his depositors are holding him responsible for their savings. He is trying to tell us that they stole all of his money too. Now you know why we really need an experienced lawman in San Juan."

"Mister Baker, I'll think on your offer and let you know. Right now I feel like my tummy has grown to my back bone. Would you like to join me for breakfast?"

"Carlen, I really need to get my store ready for the daily customers. I thank you and when it's time for supper I'll treat you."

"Mister Baker, I'll make it a point to be here when you close for the night."

The café was open, but the young lady who waited tables told him that it would be a few minutes before the coffee was ready. The place was clean and well cared for as Baker had told him. He hoped that the food was just as good.

The waitress placed a steaming cup of coffee on the table and asked what he would want for breakfast. "Young lady, I would like a pink center steak with four eggs over medium and a side bowl of gravy and a half a dozen good biscuits. I'm really hungry."

Carlen was the only customer until he was finished eating. While having a second cup of coffee five well dressed townsmen walked up to his table. Carlen rose from his chair as the five introduced themselves. Todd Simpson, the town mayor, asked, "Mister Ashton, Farris Baker brought it to our attention that you were a Texas lawman and was considering maybe to become our sheriff. We five are all members of the town council and would like to visit with you for a few minutes if you can spare us the time?"

"Why don't you gentlemen pull up a chair and have some coffee while we are talking?"

After all were seated and the waitress had their coffee on the table the mayor repeated what Baker had already told him and added a few more crimes that had been committed in their town.

"Mister Ashton, we are willing to pay you two hundred dollars per month and twenty percent of the fines that come from your office. We will furnish you an expense account and furnish you with horses, weapons and pay for your food at this café. You will be allowed to hire three deputies of your choosing at the salary of one hundred dollars per month per man. We will not hinder you in your duties and back you to the limits on what the law says is right."

"Mayor, gentlemen, your offer is very fair. I told Mister Baker that I would think it over. I would like for you to send a wire to Sheriff Henry Lang in Alice, Texas for my qualifications and his opinion of me before you consider this matter any farther. I would not try to mislead you in any way. I want you to know of my record before either you or I come to a final decision on this matter. Also I would like to have the offer you made me in print by your editor of the local newspaper with each of you a copy also. If I accept this position I want all of you to be in complete agreement with what you offer me."

The mayor replied, "Mister Ashton, I can tell that you are not just a lawman but an educated one as well. I will wire Texas this morning and have you the agreement in print by Monday morning. Can we meet you here for breakfast?"

"That will be fine with me, Mayor. I want to ride around today and get the lay of the land. I'll see all of you at daybreak Monday morning. After shaking hands the councilmen departed. Carlen asked the waitress for a refill of coffee and a piece of pie. "Sir, you must have been real hungry."

Still no one else had entered the café, so the young lady asked if she could sit and talk to him for a few minutes.

"Yes, you certainly can. I might ask you a question or two if you don't mind."

"I'll try my best to answer, Mister Ashton." "Please just call me Carlen. I'm not used to the mister."

"Alright if you will address me as Betsy, my last name is Jones. My mother and father own this eating place."

"Okay, Betsy, what would you like to talk to me about?"

"Before you take the job of sheriff I wish you would ride up on the bench and have a talk with Pete Johnson. He was the first to settle in this country and is a good honest rancher and a Texan to boot."

"Why the visit to see Mister Johnson, is he part of the town council?"

"Heavens no, that's why I would like for you to talk to him. He and Farris Baker are the two most honest men in town. I see and hear quite a lot of talk as I wait on people and I want you to get a complete picture of what you are getting yourself into."

"What you're telling me is things are not what they look like, and Pete Johnson can help me see both sides of the picture."

"Carlen, that's what I'm telling you. I'll write you a note to give Pete telling him of what's happening. You just ride on up there and talk to him."

"Okay, Betsy, write me the note and I'll be on my way."

Chapter Two

Carlen and his line back dun left town in the opposite direction of the Johnson ranch. Carlen wanted to see if someone might have decided to follow him. He headed west for a few miles where he found a low water ford, crossed the river and rode up the bank about a mile from the river and watched his back trail. After an hour he was satisfied that no one was following him. He rode east well below the town and reached the East Ridge where he first watched the town. He rode through the meadow where he had spent the night and came out on the road that led up the bluff to the bench. An hour later he dismounted at Pete Johnson's invitation and introduced himself and handed the rancher the note from Betsy Jones.

"Carlen, it sure is good to see another Texan come into our town. From what Betsy tells me in her note you have been offered the job of Sheriff. She wants me to tell you my thoughts and let you make your own decision whether you take the job or not.

"Let's go in the kitchen and have a cup of coffee while I tell you what I think."

"You sure have a nice layout here, Mister Johnson. I was raised on a ranch back home and I could tell that you were a rancher in Texas before you came here."

"Carlen, just call me Pete. I don't care for the mister part. Yes, I had a fair size spread in the north central part of the state and when the farmers came in and started building fences I decided it was time for me to move westward.

"Let me tell you my thoughts on the town council. First off I think the mayor is an honest man. The other four I have my doubts about. Vernon Hull is the town banker and is from the New England area. He came in here about three years ago and started up the bank. He is a slick talker and is a single man who keeps to himself and is not what I call a friendly person.

"Winfred Barnett owns the Brown Mule Saloon. He is in cahoots with the banker on several deals like buying and selling horses and cattle along with some real estate in the general area.

"Grady Holmes lives in town but owns a ranch on the Utah border. He runs a rough crew of men that I would class as outlaws. He has a lot of dealings with the banker too.

"Giles Farnsworth is a land agent for the government and he is in thick with the banker also. You never see them all together, but I have first hand information that they are thick as fleas on a dog's back in some shady deals."

"Pete, I wanted to come west just to go back to being a cowboy. What you're telling me makes me wonder about your cattle being stolen and the bank being robbed. I might just take the job of sheriff and see if I can tie these four jaspers up with these and other things that are happening around the town of San Juan. I need men to be my deputies that I can trust. I may have to call on you and some of your crew if I can locate where these rustlers hang out."

"Carlen, me and my cowboys will help you in any way we can. I have a couple of hands that I don't trust too much and I'm not going to tell anybody anything until you give me the word that you need us. I can think of only one man that would make you a fine deputy and I will talk to him the first time I see him. His name is William Rose, but we all just call him Bill. He is very level headed and good with pistol or rifle and has no fear of man or beast.

"There is a lawyer in town by the name of Curtiss Fletcher. He is a fellow that you need to meet and make friends with. He isn't very fond of the four council members we have been discussing. He handles what little legal work I have and we have had a few discussions on how they handle their affairs."

"Well, Pete, it has been my pleasure meeting you and I'll keep you posted. We best act like we don't know each other and I'll get in touch with you through Betsy. I promised Farris Baker that I would meet him for supper so I'd better hit the road or he'll think I've forgottten him."

"Carlen, the minute you put on that badge you keep a sharp eye out because there are a few people around here that doesn't want San Juan to have another lawman in town."

"I'll be sure and keep my eyes peeled for any and all trouble. Thanks again Pete and I'll be in touch as soon as I find out anything."

Carlen tied his mount to the rail in front of the general store and entered to see Farris waiting on a young lady that looked like she just stepped from the pages of a lady's magazine. He thought her to be around twenty two years old. She was wearing a blue dress that showed her feminine figure and her black hair reached to her tiny waist. Carlen never thought too much about the opposite sex but this lady would catch any man's eye. Well, he had too much on his mind to even think about a pretty lady.

Farris wrapped her purchase and thanked her and as she passed Carlen he removed his hat and gave her a slight bow as she smiled and went through the open door.

"Farris, are you about ready to close up and have that supper we talked about?"

"Let me lock up today's receipts in the safe and I'll be ready."

Carlen watched the street while the store keeper went to the office in the back of the store and locked up his money and charge tickets. Farris left his apron on the front counter and locked up the front door and said, "Carlen, I would like to treat you to this meal."

Carlen couldn't help but like the store keeper. He was as friendly as a person could be. Evidently the folks in San Juan gave him all of their business as the only other store in town was not near the size as the San Juan Emporium and probably didn't carry half as much merchandise.

Betsy was cleaning off a table where two other customers had just finished eating when they walked in. She greeted them with a smile and told them to have a seat and she would serve them in just a minute. Carlen figured Farris had a place that he always sat and he followed him to the corner table close to the kitchen door. "I always try to sit here, Carlen, it saves a few steps for Betsy, and Lord knows she walks quite a few miles in here every day except Sunday."

The young lady set two iced glasses of water on the table and asked if they were ready for supper.

"Farris, I guess that you want the same thing you always have."

"No, Betsy, I'm treating my friend Carlen and I think we should have something special tonight. Carlen, is there anything special on the menu that you would like to order?"

"Farris, I'm not very choosy, why don't you order for both of us?"

"Very well. Betsy, please bring us a good beef steak with mashed potatoes covered with cream gravy and some pinto beans. I hope you still have some of the sourdough bread."

"We always do, Farris. I guess you want sweetened ice tea to drink."

"That would be fine. Then we will have a slice of pie each with coffee for dessert."

When Betsy left for their order Farris asked what he thought of the offer the city council made him.

"I told them I would give it a lot of thought and give them my answer Monday morning here at breakfast. I really had my heart set on just being a cowboy but I can see from what the mayor told me that San Juan really needs a dependable lawman."

"Carlen, you are a young man and I can tell that you are mature more than your years show. I'm sure that you can handle the job but I don't want to see you get wounded or killed. This country is a long way from being peaceful and there are some really rough, mean characters around here. There are only a few people around here that you can depend on or trust. Pete Johnson is getting on in years but he is honest and solid as a rock. Curtiss Fletcher is a lawyer here in town and I believe he is really a trustworthy fellow. Our mayor, Todd Simpson, is dependable but the other four council members pretty well run things. You will have a hard time bucking them."

"Farris, did you lose your money too when the bank was robbed?"

"No, I never trusted Vernon Hull when he first come to town and started the bank. I always keep my funds in the large safe I ordered from Saint Louis when I first opened up here. I had been warned that bank robbery was a common occurrence in these isolated little towns. Pete Johnson leaves his money with me too."

"Farris, I believe that one day or night soon someone will try to bust your safe or force you to open it. I've seen this happen three times while I was a deputy in Texas. You have the largest business in the area and I suppose most of the people you give credit pay their accounts off around the first of the month. That's usually the time the robbery will occur."

"I doubt, Carlen, if anyone could bust that big safe open."

"Don't you ever doubt they can't, if dynamite won't work then they will force you to open it at the point of a gun barrel."

"You know that I've never thought of anything like that happening to me."

"Farris, with the bank no longer in business you will be the only place in town that has a safe place for the people to keep their funds. Let me ask you if you know where the saloon keeper Winfred Barnett keeps his money?"

"I have no idea, Carlen. I guess that he has a safe of some kind in his place of business. What made you ask me of this?"

"Well, Farris, the saloon does a total cash business and he is bound to keep a lot of cash on hand. I just wondered if he kept any money in the bank when it was robbed."

"I've seen him go into the bank a few times but I can't remember him caring a money sack of any kind."

Carlen watched Betsy starting to bring their food from the kitchen and told Farris not to tell anyone what they talked about. Farris agreed.

Farris paid Betsy for the food and Carlen left her a generous tip.

"That sure was a good supper, Farris, and I enjoyed your company. The next one is on me. I guess I'd better stable my horse and see if I can find a room for the night. Where did the last sheriff in town live?"

"He stayed at the hotel what little time he was sheriff. He wasn't what I would call an industrious fellow. He just went with the flow. I don't think he had any kin around here and he wasn't a real friendly fellow at all."

"I'll come by the store after the meeting Monday morning and let you know how things turn out with the council members."

Carlen rode his dun to the stable and told the hostler that he would tend to the horse himself. The stable owner was an older fellow and was as friendly as Farris. He had gotten wind of Carlen being asked to become the sheriff of San Juan and told him if he took the job that he would make sure that he would keep his best horses for him to use.

The hotel desk clerk welcomed him to his establishment and fixed him up with a room on the second floor. He told Carlen he would have his bath water up to his room in a few minutes.

Carlen got comfortable on the feather bed and put his thoughts to the meeting that he was to attend Monday morning. He knew that some of the council members didn't like it when he wanted the printed offer from the newspaper editor. He made up his mind if they didn't have it worded like the mayor said he would, then he would not accept the offer.

The five councilmen arrived while Carlen was on his second cup of coffee. He stood as they each pulled up a chair and waited until they were seated before he sat down. The mayor asked if he had come to a decision yet and Carlen asked if he had the printed offer with him.

"Yes, I also have a reply from Sheriff Lang in Texas. Mister Lang has given you a very high recommendation, I might add. He said that you were the best and most dependable man that he ever worked with."

"Mayor, may I have a copy of the printed proposal?"

The mayor withdrew a folded paper from his inside coat pocket and handed it to him.

Carlen unfolded the letter and read it to himself and said, "Mayor, gentlemen, since this is not the offer you gave me verbally Saturday, I cannot accept the position of sheriff."

The mayor was shocked and asked, "I gave the editor exactly what we proposed to you. I haven't read it so let's go over it and see where the mistake is."

"Mayor, the verbal agreement you gave me was that I could hire three deputies of my own choice. This printed copy states that any and all deputies will be hired by the town council.

"If I'm going to have the responsibility of the office of sheriff I fully intend to hire and fire my choice of who I'm to be responsible for. Thank you for your time and effort, but I'm not interested in the offer you have made. Good day gentlemen."

Carlen rose from his seat and paid Betsy for his breakfast and left for his hotel room.

It wasn't but just a few minutes until there was a knock on his door. Carlen opened the door and the mayor asked, "Carlen, may I come in and talk with you for a few minutes?"

"Sure, come in, Mayor, but there is no use of you trying to get me to be your sheriff."

"Carlen, I don't know how or why the editor changed the wording of the hand written paper that I gave him. I can assure you that I wrote down just what I offered you before I made you the offer. It was the same paper I gave the editor."

"I can tell you exactly why it was changed and who told the editor to change the wording."

"You mean that the editor didn't change for his own reasons?"

"No, Mayor, one or more of your town council members had one of their hired hands tell him to do it and not to reveal to anyone that he told him to do so."

"Carlen, why would any of them want to do that?"

"Pull up that chair and have a seat Mayor, and I'll try to explain, but what I'm telling you can go no farther than this room. If it does I'm marked for a bullet in my back."

"You really are serious about this aren't you Carlen?"

"Yes, Mayor, I'm very serious. I know if you breathe a word of what I'm going to tell you we both will be marked for death.

"First off, the editor was probably told that if he told who made him change the wording he would be killed. The man who told him was employed by one or more of your city council members. The reason is they want to place one of their own in as a deputy so they will have an inside track to whatever the sheriff plans or who is under suspicion on anything they think might involve them in anyway. I would bet you that the last sheriff you had in office, one or more of his deputies was picked by the council. Am I correct?"

The mayor's grim look on his face told Carlen that he was correct. "Yes, Carlen, but how do you know all of these things?"

"Because I'm a trained lawman, Mayor. What I have told you I'll tell you again not to repeat a word of what we have discussed."

"You need not worry about me saying anything to anyone, not even my wife or daughter. I never dreamed of anything like this going on in San Juan."

"Think back, Mayor, of who has come to town here in the past few years and you will, in your own mind, figure out when all of the trouble here started. Then you might see things a little different."

"Carlen, what am I going to do? I have no idea of where to turn or who I may go to for help. It's not only the town, but all of the ranchers and the few farmers here in our county that are worried to death. I thought that you would be the answer to my prayers, but I can see why you won't take the job and I can't blame you."

"Mayor, just keep on like you have been, don't let the other council members suspect a thing. Just keep calm and I can promise you that I will do something to help you and the good folks here. I'll put a stop to whoever is behind this. I may have to leave town for a few days but I'll be back and still will not be your sheriff. I'll come back just as a plain cowhand and if we talk then it will have to be somewhere besides here in town."

"Carlen, I'll do everything I can to help you in any way that I can. Is there any way that you can get in touch with me without anyone knowing about it?"

"Yes, Mayor, just pretend that nothing has changed. When I can I'll get word to you through another party that I can trust."

The mayor extended his hand and Carlen smiled and shook hands with him. He told him just to remain calm and forget what they had discussed.

Chapter Three

Carlen walked around the town just looking in the windows. When he saw the barber shop he went in and spent a few minutes getting a haircut, which he needed very badly.

He waited until the few customers left the San Juan Emporium. He didn't want to bother Farris while he was busy. Carlen opened the front door and heard the tinkle of the bell again. Farris was sweeping up a spot of flour that someone had spilled. He looked up and grinned when he saw it was Carlin.

"Well, Son, I've already got the word that you turned down the job of sheriff of our bustling metropolis. I was hoping they would talk you into trying to serve us, but I can't blame you at all for not taking the job. Carlen, I've been putting some thought into hiring some help lately. I can't offer you the kind of money that the town council did, but I can pay you a whole lot more than a cowboy would make and the work is not near as hard."

"Farris, I just might take you up on that offer in a few days but first I have a couple of things that I have to take care of. Do you know the attorney, Curtiss, here in town?"

"Sure I do. He stops by nearly every day at lunch and we shoot the bull for a few minutes. Curtiss is a good fellow. Some judge up in Durango helped him through school and suggested he come here to start his practice. We had no lawyer here and really needed one. I want you to meet him Carlen, he is about your age and is smart as a whip."

"I sure would like that, Farris. I'll come back around about lunch time and if he's here you can introduce me to him. "

As Carlen walked out to the plank walk Farris called again for him to think real hard about the job offer. Carlen told him he would.

Carlen spent an hour in the café drinking coffee and talking with Betsy when she didn't have a customer. He spoke to her of Curtiss Fletcher. She told him that she had been to the last three town dances with him and he was really a gentleman and she was very fond of him.

He spent the next hour in his room and put together his thoughts on how was the best way to do the job he wanted to without being a lawman. He had several opportunities to become a U.S. Deputy Marshal and wished that he was one now. He could work without a badge on his shirt and could not let anyone know his position until he was ready to make the arrest. The only problem was that he would have no help that he could depend on except Pete Johnson. Pete's ranch was a three hour ride there and back and time was always a factor.

He opened the tinkle bell door on Farris's store and a man about his age was sitting on the store counter talking with Farris. "Curtiss, I want you to meet Carlen Ashton." The lawyer slipped from the counter and offered his hand and said, "Carlen, I am proud to meet you. I've been talking to Farris and he has told me that you turned down the job as our county sheriff."

"It's a pleasure to meet you also, Curtiss. Yes, I turned the town council down. I've been thinking about the job Farris has asked me to take helping him in the store."

The bell tinkled again and two ladies came in with a list in their hand for Farris. Farris said, "If you boys want to talk just go back there in my office while I wait on these fine ladies."

Carlen told Curtiss of the reason that he would not accept the position of sheriff but did not speak of his conversation with the mayor.

"Curtiss, where is the closest office for the U.S. Marshal's service located?"

"There used to be one in Durango which is about a three days ride from here. The marshal force there cleaned up the four corners area and last year the last marshal retired. The only office in the state is in Denver. I know the judge in Durango. He helped me get through law school and suggested that I start my practice here as there were no legal services in this area. I'm sure that Judge Hayes could be of help to you. If you like I can give you a letter explaining all of our troubles here."

"I would really appreciate any help you and the judge could give me. I have a good idea of what's going on here and I would really like to help put a stop to it. There are some really good folks in San Juan and I would like to settle down here. I've seen too much of this kind of people who want to control the town and county in the five years I served as a lawman in Texas. Write me the letter for the judge and I'll head for Durango."

Curtiss used the pen and paper on the desk in Farris's office and penned a two page letter and handed it to Carlen and said, "Carlen, we had better keep this just between the two of us. I know that there are a few people around here that would try to kill you before you got to Durango."

"I'm well aware of that, Curtiss, so I'll get going right now. I hope the people who are involved in these robberies and murder think I'm gone for good."

Carlen noticed that Farris was still trying to fill the orders for the two ladies so he just gave him a wave and went to the hotel and checked out. With his rifle in his right hand and his small war bag over his shoulder he headed straight to the livery for his line back dun. Saddled up and riding east down main street he watched as Betsy came out on the plank walk and waved him a goodbye. He returned the wave and hoped that he could accomplish something on his trip to see the judge in Durango.

Late that afternoon as he watched for a good place to camp for the night, he caught a flash of sunlight from a rifle barrel. He rolled off the right side of his mount and was pulling his Winchester from the saddle boot when he heard the sound of the rifle. He slid behind a large rock and watched the place where the shot came from. A man stood up and was looking in his direction, thinking that his shot had killed Carlen. The big dun horse had not moved since Carlen rolled out of the saddle. This was blocking out the shooter's view and he started walking down the hill to make sure that his bullet had knocked Carlen off his mount. Carlen hated to have to kill the man but this was a life or death struggle and he wanted to live. When the man raised the rifle to kill the big horse Carlen shot him. The man was knocked over backwards and dropped the rifle. Carlen walked over to the man who was breathing in rapid grasps for air. He removed the man's pistol and asked him, "Who paid you to kill me?"

Blood was starting to foam in bubbles as the man tried to speak. Carlen watched his eyes glaze over and after a quick shudder the man was dead. Carlen searched him and found ten gold eagles in his pockets. There was nothing else besides an old pocket knife. He mounted his horse and rode up to where the man shot at him from, and in a few minutes found where he had tied a sorrel mare. She had a feed bag on to keep her from nickering if she smelled Carlen's big dun. Searching the saddle bags the only thing he found was a running iron and some pigging strings. He removed the nose bag and placed it in the saddle bag and put the pigging strings in his pocket with the coins. Leading the mare back to the dead man, he tightened the saddle girt and tied the man belly down across the saddle. He knew that the horse would go back to where ever it came from. After tying the man's feet and hands to the stirrups he wound his rope around him so there was no chance of him falling from the mare. He removed the bridle and tied it with the reins to the saddle horn and slapped the mare. She trotted off a few yards and started in a southwest direction. Carlen thought once about following her but since she wore no brand he decided against it. Night was coming and it would be easy to lose the trail in the dark.

Two days later he rode down the streets of Durango. Carlen thought that this was as nice of a town that he had ever seen. The streets were clean and everything was in an orderly fashion. He knew that it was too late to try to see Judge Hayes, so he got a room for the night and stabled his horse. In the hotel dining room he found directions to the building where the judge had his office. The next morning, bathed and shaved, he decided to walk instead of saddling up. He knew it might be a long wait before he could get a time to meet with the judge.

It was a longer walk than he expected it to be. The sign on the front of the building told him that this was a Federal Court-house. He entered the three story brick building and found that the office he was seeking was on the second floor. Climbing the stairs he read the gold letters on the frosted glass door. Federal Judge R.L. Hayes. Carlen knocked on the door and an older lady with her hair tied in a tight bun on the back of her head opened the door and asked him in. She asked if he was here on court business. He told her that he had a letter from Curtiss Fletcher that he was to deliver personally to Judge Hayes.

"Just have a seat young man and I'll see if Judge Hayes can see you now. He has a light schedule today and court will not be held until two this afternoon."

Carlen took a seat in one of the un-cushioned chairs thinking he would have a long wait. Just as he settled and crossed his legs the lady came from the other room and told him to come with her. They crossed a long room with a large table surrounded by chairs like the one he was sitting in. He figured that this was the jurors ante room. At the other end of the room she opened the door and told Carlen the judge would see him now.

His Honor rose from behind his large desk and extended his hand to Carlen and introductions were made. The judge told him to have a seat.

"Carlen, I understand that you have a letter from a young man that I admire."

"Yes, Sir, I do. Curtiss Fletcher asked me to deliver this to you as I need to speak with you about a problem in San Juan."

Carlen passed the letter to the Judge and His Honor unfolded it and took his time to read it thoroughly. "Carlen, I have heard a few rumors of things down there, but this is the first time I realized that things were going from bad to worse."

"Sir, I have a very good Idea who are the ones behind all of these robberies and murder. The first day I left to come here to meet you there was an attempt on my life. I was forced to kill the man who shot at me and I found no identification on his person or in his saddle bags. The only things he carried with him was a running iron and ten new gold eagles. One or more of the men who serve on the city council had reason to fear me. They knew my record as a lawman and the reason I would not accept the position as their county sheriff. I left San Juan within three hours of my refusal that they offered me. I need some legal authority and a month or more of undercover work. If I'm not killed in the process I believe I can have all of this brought to court and stopped."

"Carlen, you remind me of a young man a few years back that I swore in as the first U.S. Marshal in the four corners area. I need confirmation of your duty as a deputy and of your service before I can pin a marshal's badge on you. Give me the name and place of the sheriff that you served under and come back to see me right after lunch and I should have the wire back from him by then."

Carlen gave the judge the information that he asked for and thanked him for his time and effort to help him.

At one o'clock sharp the judge entered the door to his office and smiled when he looked at Carlen seated and waiting for his return. "Come on into my chambers and let's look at what Sheriff Lang sent me in reply to my questions." Again they were in the same two chairs as they had sat in before.

"Carlen, I understand from the sheriff you worked under in Texas that you could well fill the position that I'm going to offer you. I know that there is always a danger of my losing a marshal but that is the risk that you have to take. I know from what Curtiss has written about your concern for the law that is needed in San Juan. The report from Sheriff Lang tells me in his wire that you are the person that takes his job very serious. The long trip up here also tells me that the law is the thing you are concerned about most. I'm going to swear you in as a U.S. Marshal and give you a badge and a power of attorney to hire you a deputy marshal if and when you feel there is need for one. You will be on the federal payroll as of today and will stay on it until you resign or I feel as though you are not performing your duty. The deputy will be your responsibility to discharge when you are finished with the problems in San Juan County. The main office for the marshals happens to be in Denver, but it is in my power to place qualified lawmen into service as they are needed. I closed this marshal's office when my last marshal retired a year ago.

"Now, raise your right hand and repeat after me." Judge Hayes administered the oath to Carlen then handed him the two badges and a power of attorney. "Marshal Ashton, if you need me or anything that I can help you with just send me a coded message to Little River Stables here in Durango. Should you need help just place the words black horse in part of the message. Also you can write me at the address but be careful and make sure that the letter will be in code also. Write me if you need funds and I will send a rider to meet you wherever you say."

"Your Honor, I'm planning to go to work in the San Juan Emporium general store and will most likely be wearing an apron to show the town that I'm about as far from being an officer of the law that I can. Tell your messenger that if I'm not there to tell Farris Baker that he is friend of Curtiss Fletcher. Farris will send him to Curtiss and I'll explain this to him."

"Carlen, I see that you have already got your plans thought out. I wish you well and by all means possible take care of yourself." Carlen thanked the judge, shook his extended hand and headed to the livery stable to saddle up and be on his way.

Chapter Four

Carlen rode south following the Animas River until late afternoon when he crossed the river and turned south by southwest. At sundown he built a small fire and made a small pot of coffee. He ate a sandwich that he had purchased along with a few other things before leaving Durango. After finishing his meal he put out the fire and rode on until after dark and had a cold camp for the night. Early the next morning he was on his way. One longer day and another night put him at Pete Johnson's ranch in time to have a noon meal with him. He couldn't tell Pete that he was a marshal, but did tell him that he was going to try to find out who exactly was behind all of the trouble in the county. He also told him he was going to use the job that Farris offered him as a cover.

"Pete, I just couldn't take the job as sheriff with the members of the town council hiring the deputies that could just be spies for the outlaws."

"I understand that, Carlen, and I don't blame you. I guess that if and when you find out who the top culprits are that it's me and you that are going to have to clean this mess up."

"Pete, I sure would like to talk to this fellow Bill Rose on the quiet side just to feel him out. I think if he wants to he could be a lot of help to both of us."

"I'll see him in a couple of days and tell him to drop by the store and you can tell him to meet you after dark where you two can be alone."

"That will work. Just be sure that only you and I know what's going on. If the word was to leak out they would be ready to kill both of us."

"You can trust me on that, Carlen, and Bill Rose is a man you can really count on too."

"Well, Pete, I guess I'd better get to town and see if Farris has an apron that will fit me."

"Carlen, you just take good care of yourself son. I sure don't want anything to happen to you for trying to help us here in San Juan County. "

Carlen stabled his mount and after caring for him booked a room for the night in the hotel. The desk clerk told him it was good to have him as a guest again and hoped that he had reconsidered the job as sheriff. Carlen told the young man that he might become a clerk for Farris at his store, but that he wasn't interested in being sheriff. He got his bath and shaved.

He had supper at the café where Vernon Hull, the banker, sat talking with a rough looking man dressed in range clothes wearing a shell belt with a pistol in the tied down holster. The two gave Carlen a hard look and he had the feeling that they suspected that he had killed the man on the trail to Durango.

Betsy gave him a smile and said, "Carlen, we all thought you had left town for good."

"Well, I went to see a man about a job, but Farris had offered me a better deal to go to work for him. I thought that being a clerk for him might be an easier job than punching cows, so here I am. I hope that Farris hasn't filled the position yet or I will be leaving for good."

The banker and his cowhand or gunny got up and paid out. They left without speaking. Farris was entering as they met at the door and when Farris greeted them the banker just nodded. Farris joined Carlen at his favorite table and asked if he was ready to go to work for him.

"I can start in the morning if you still need a hand, Farris."

"Well, let's have supper and we'll talk it over. Betsy, I guess that I'll have the same thing that I always eat."

Carlen looked at Betsy and shook his head, "No, Betsy, It's my time to buy and we will have the same things that we had when Farris picked up the tab, if that is okay with him."

"It's fine with me, Carlen, I don't eat that high on the hog very often, but since you are going to work for me I'll just take you up on it."

Carlen was waiting at the front door of the store when Farris arrived the next morning to unlock and get ready for his first day of work. Carlen asked for an apron then took the broom and started sweeping the plank walk clean. After that was finished he started on the huge store. An hour later he started dusting the shelves. He was cleaning off the sales counter when the bell on the front door tinkled. He looked up and the first customer of the day happened to be the pretty lady with the long black hair he had seen once before. She greeted him with a smile and he asked, "Good morning to you young lady. May I help you?"

"I hope so. I need to purchase a small pistol that I can carry in my purse. There has been a man following me ever since I came here two weeks ago and I am afraid of him. I can't understand why he watches me all of the time. I have talked to my brother about him but he just laughs and told me that no one in the west would bother a lady."

"Maybe the man thinks that you are single and he hopes to meet you. There are a very few single ladies in the west and a lot of men are looking for a wife. There are very few men that would harm a woman out here because he would be hung by other men without a trial. Just the same there is always the chance that this man wants to do you harm. Let me show you what we have that would fit your needs."

Carlen showed her a small double barrel derringer and explained how it worked. He placed a forty one caliber bullet in each barrel to show her how to load the weapon, then removed them and instructed her how to pull the trigger. "You pull the trigger once and the top barrel fires then pull it again and the other fires. This is a short range weapon and it's not made for accuracy. If anyone tries to harm you just point it in the center of their chest and shoot. This little pistol is carried by a lot of women and shoots hard enough to kill a person at close range."

The lady asked, "Could you teach me how to shoot it after work this afternoon?"

"Yes, I would be happy to. It makes quite a bang and it will scare you the first few times you shoot it. After you become familiar with the weapon it will be a good companion to you. This is my first day at work here and I don't know for sure when closing time is. If you can tell me where I can find you I'll be there as soon as we close. We need to get away from town to do the shooting. I'll rent a buggy and pick you up. It shouldn't take long to teach you."

"I really appreciate you doing this for me. My name is Peggy Fletcher and I'm staying with my brother, Curtiss. I will be the new school teacher here as soon as school opens up after the summer recess is over."

"I'm Carlen Ashton, Miss Fletcher, and I'm acquainted with your brother and Curtiss can accompany us if he likes."

She paid Carlen for the pistol and a box of fifty shells and told him that she would be ready when he arrived.

The day passed without a lot of customers and Farris told him that the week days were usually slow except Friday afternoons. Saturday is always our busiest day. Nearly everyone in the county come to town to visit and stock up on what supplies they need for the next week.

"On the first Saturday of every month there is a social and dance at the community center. You might ask Curtiss's sister if you could escort her this Saturday night. She is a very attractive young lady and you two seem to hit it right off. I know that all of the cowboys will be after her."

"Farris, do you think for a minute that she would go to the dance with a man who wears an apron to work?"

"Why don't you ask her and find out? By the way I want to show you to your quarters."

Carlen followed him to the back of the large building and opened a door across the hall from his office. "You can have this apartment at no cost and there is a bath in behind the bedroom. I had it built as I was having the store built to use for myself. I fooled around and got married and purchased a nice home across the river. My wife died two years ago and the place has never been lived in."

"Farris, I sure appreciate this. I could not ask for any anything nicer or cleaner. I just hope that I can make you the clerk you want me to be."

"Carlen, I know that you are a lawman at heart and I expect after you clean this county up I'll lose you. I have no idea of what you have planned but I have got the feeling that you are going to do it one way or another. I talked to Pete Johnson and told him my feelings and he told me that he felt the same way. Pete is just like me, no wife or no children. We are a couple of lonesome old birds. I knew that you were a good man the first morning that you walked in my front door and I trust you and enjoy your company. Now go rent that buggy and teach Miss Fletcher how to shoot that little pistol you sold her."

Carlen helped the hostler rig out the single seat buggy and he told him where to go to give the young lady a shooting lesson. Carlen knew that Farris had let him off a little early from work and that he wanted him to get well acquainted with Peggy Fletcher.

He knocked on the door to the Fletcher home and Curtiss opened the door and asked him in. "Carlen, sis told me that you sold her a pistol today and you are going to give her a few pointers on how to handle the weapon. "

"Curtiss, I can't really think badly of her wanting the little pistol and I hope she never has to use it. In case she needs to I want her to know how to use and care for it and the safety measures she needs to take."

"Well my friend, I don't think that she could find a better teacher. She is dressing now and will be ready in a few minutes."

"Curtiss, there may be a fellow by the name of Bill Rose come to visit you in a day or two and you and I need to have a talk with him. He was recommended to me by Pete Johnson. I hate to get you anymore involved in this situation but you are the only one in town that really knows what we are trying to accomplish."

"I know Bill and also know that he is a very trustworthy person. When he makes contact with me I'll arrange for the three of us to meet after dark where we can have some privacy."

Peggy came from her bedroom all dressed in regular cowboy range wear. "Carlen, I guess I'm ready to become a lady shootist. I know that most ladies don't go around wearing men's clothing but if I'm going to live in the west I want to dress the part."

"You look very fine to me, Miss Fletcher, and if I was you I wouldn't care what some of the other people might think."

"Carlen, my name is Peggy and I would like it very much if you would address me as Peggy instead of being so formal."

Curtiss spoke, "Carlen, you might as well get use to my sister and know that she has a mind of her own."

"Well, if you two can stop jabbering we will get this first lesson for me on its way."

"You two gun toting cowboys be sure you don't shoot yourselves in the foot."

Carlen helped Peggy into the buggy seat and headed east toward the curve in the river. He tied the mare to a small cottonwood tree to make sure that the noise from the pistol wouldn't scare her off.

Lightning had, at one time, struck a large cottonwood tree and all that was left was a stump about six feet high. Carlen told her to load up the derringer and stay about five feet from the stump. "Don't try to aim the pistol just point it like it is an extension of your pointing finger and squeeze the trigger one time. Be careful to keep the weapon pointed at the stump after the shot."

He watched carefully as she placed two bullets in the barrels then snapped it shut and raised the weapon and fired the top barrel. The little pistol made an awful loud noise but she controlled it well and still had it pointed on the stump. "Now, release the trigger and squeeze it again." Smoke belched from the barrel and again the loud bang occurred.

"Now, Peggy, break the barrels and reload again." She quickly reloaded and snapped it shut, raised the weapon and fired two more shots. She then lowered the weapon and walked to the stump and counted the four bullet holes. Carlen looked and then told her that she should be giving him shooting lesson instead of him trying to show her how to shoot. He explained how to clean the weapon and how important it was to keep it clean.

"Carlen, I really want to thank you for taking the time to help me. I'm not accustomed to a lot of the ways of the west and I fully intend to lean on you for help and instructions. I hear that this Saturday night there is a social and dance at the community center. I am expecting you to take me, as I know there isn't anyone else who would put up with an old maid school teacher."

"Peggy, I would consider it my pleasure to escort you. The only thing I have to fear is all of the cowboys will never let me have one dance with you. If you think that you are an old maid school teacher, I must be an older bachelor lawman."

"I' thought that you were a clerk working for Mister Baker."

"I am as of today. In Texas I was a lawman for five years. Now I am just an apron wearing store clerk with no experience of the job I am hired to do."

"Well, I'm thankful that you're not a lawman anymore. I think that is the most dangerous kind of work that a person could do."

"Peggy, if it wasn't for lawmen, what do you think the country would be like? These men risk their lives every day so the honest people can have the thought of security in their community. You will find here in the west that there are a thousand more outlaws than there is one officer of the law. I don't know where you grew up but life here on the frontier is totally different than back in the eastern towns and cities."

"I really never put much thought into the matter, Carlen. I thought things here would be just like they were in Tennessee where I was born and raised. I guess that I have so much to learn about the west and the people here."

"Well, Miss School Teacher, since its supper time, how about me treating you to a good steak?"

"Mister Clerk, I happily accept your offer and this Friday night before the social I'll have your supper cooked at my abode and will be expecting you to dine with me."

"You couldn't keep me away with a shotgun. I'll be there with bells on."

After delivering Peggy home, Carlen helped the hostler put the buggy away and tended to the gentle mare.

Chapter Five

Carlen had checked out of the hotel and moved his belongings to the apartment in the large store. The next morning he was the first customer in the San Juan café. Betsy set his coffee on the table that he and Farris claimed as their private property and told her that he would wait for his boss. In a few minutes Farris entered and with a good morning to everyone. He sat with Carlen and told Betsy that he would take his usual short stack of pancakes with a side order of bacon cooked crisp. "Well, Carlen, how did the shooting lesson go?"

"She can shoot as good as a lot of men I know. I just watched as she put four slugs into a tree stump. I could cover the slugs she put in the stump with one hand."

"I don't suppose that you asked her to go to the dance with you?"

"No, I didn't have to. She gave me orders that she expected me to take her. I told her that you wouldn't let me and she pulled that little pistol out of her purse and said she would have a talk with you today about giving me orders like that."

Betsy laughed as Farris's chin dropped and he looked like a whipped puppy. He finally realized that Carlen was just pulling his leg and joined the laughter. "Well, Son, I guess that you will have to get fitted out with some fancy duds to wear. We don't want you to go looking like one of these range riders around here."

"Farris, I've worked one day for you and now you want me to go in debt for something special to wear to a Saturday night cowboy dance."

"Well, I guess I can give you a little discount since you are an employee. You can pay me back in a year or two."

When they entered the store and were ready for the days customers, Farris picked a nice black suit with a white shirt and a string tie and told Carlen to go try them on to see if they fit.

They did, and Farris wrapped them and told Carlen he would be gone a few minutes. Carlen stuck his head out of the front door and watched Farris deliver the bundle of clothes to the Chinese laundry down the street. Farris didn't want him to go to the dance in a shelf wrinkled suit. Carlen knew that Farris had taken him under his wing. He thought a lot of Farris.

Friday night Carlen knocked on the door of the Fletcher residence and Peggy opened the door and bid him to enter. On the white cloth over the kitchen table were three lighted candles and two place settings with silverware placed on red napkins. "Have a seat on the sofa and I'll have supper on the table in a couple of minutes."

"Where is my friend, Curtiss?"

"I told him that this supper was for the two of us and for him to go spend the evening with Betsy."

The meal was perfect. She could shoot and she could cook. He wondered if she could ride a horse.

After the meal was finished Carlen helped her with the dishes. He knew that he had never met a woman that could compare to her self reliance and her beauty. He knew that when she learned the real reason of his mission that he would lose her. If she only understood what had to be done to make San Juan a decent and safe place to live.

The couple sat in the porch swing and enjoyed the other's company while they waited for Curtiss to return. Peggy was an easy woman to talk to. She was very down to earth and well educated. Carlen knew that she was one in a million. The only thing she needed was a real understanding of the frontier and the people who braved the hardships to tame it.

Curtiss arrived around midnight and Carlen told Peggy again how much he enjoyed the supper and her wonderful companionship. "Carlen, you be sure and pick me up at seven tomorrow evening for the social and dance."

"I'll be here on time if Farris will not try to stay open until the sun comes up."

Saturday was a busy day, as Farris told him. The day passed swiftly and at six Farris locked the front door as the last customer left and flipped the sign on the window to read closed. Carlen had told the hostler at the livery stable that he wanted the buggy ready to go by six forty five. He bathed, shaved and was on his way to the stable by six thirty. The hostler had the rig all clean and had placed a lap blanket on the seat.

Carlen thanked the man and headed toward the Fletcher residence. He dropped the anchor weight to hold the mare and knocked on the front door. Curtiss answered and told him that Peggy was almost ready and that he was going to pick up Betsy and would see them there.

Peggy came onto the porch dressed in a white dress with lace collar and sleeves. She was more beautiful each time he looked at her. "You are one minute late, Carlen."

"I've been here for the past ten minutes waiting on you. Besides your house clock is a minute fast. I must tell you that you look stunning. All of the cowboys will surround you and if I get to dance with you it will be a miracle."

"Oh hush, you're just trying to butter me up like a whiskey drummer baits the bartender he is trying to sell his rotgut to."

She patted Carlen on the arm and when he looked at her she gave him a big smile and promised him the first and last dance.

The community hall was full and there were ladies serving cookies and punch at a long table on the far side of the room. The musicians were tuning their instruments and the men were picking their partners. A group of cowboys made for Peggy and she took Carlen by the hand and told them that this was his dance. The band played a waltz and Peggy felt light as a feather as they glided across the floor. Carlen knew that the cowboys were going to pester her all night and he was thankful that he got the first dance. The music ended and Carlen gave her a Texas bow when the group of range riders came again. Carlen backed away as a gentleman should do to show courtesy to his date.

He got a glass of punch and backed against the wall watching the dancers when he felt a tug at his sleeve. Curtiss motioned for him to follow as they went out on the back patio. The light was dim and Carlen made out a man standing in the shadows between two oleander bushes.

"Carlen, I want you to meet Bill Rose." They exchanged a firm handshake and Carlen told him that Pete Johnson wanted them to meet.

"Bill, I want to sit down with you and bring you up to date on what I'm trying to do for the people of San Juan County. I don't think that this is the place to talk or be seen together. I have an apartment in Farris Baker's store. If you can come to the loading dock, there is a walk in door beside the large double doors. Knock three times and I'll let you in. I would like for Curtiss to be with us so he will know all that we talk about. I have Curtiss's sister here and just as soon as the dance and social are over I will take her home and put the buggy back in the livery stable. I would appreciate it if you two will meet me then at the store."

Curtiss told them that the party would end at eleven o'clock and that they would be there around eleven thirty. Bill stuck out his hand and said, "Carlen, it is a pleasure to meet you and I will do anything that I can to help rid this county of this bunch of crooks. I'll be there with Curtiss."

The last dance was another waltz for most of the dancers were tired and ready to finish. Peggy kept her word and reached out to Carlen. "Some of these cowhands don't think that I have any feet. I have never had my toes stepped on so many times at one dance." The slow waltz started and Peggy placed her head on his shoulder and relaxed as Carlen held her firmly as they glided across the floor. He guided her toward the door and when the music stopped he felt her arm slip into his as they walked to the buggy. All of the way home she was up against his right side with her head resting on his shoulder. He dropped the anchor weight and lifted her out of the buggy and assisted her to the front door. She then placed the key in the lock and opened the door then turned and kissed him on the cheek and told him thanks for the two dances they had together. "I'll drop in at the store and see you sometime Monday."

"If you can, come by around one in the afternoon and I'll buy our lunch."

"That will be fine." Then she kissed him on the other cheek and told him goodnight.

Carlen dropped the buggy off with the hostler and thanked him for being so prompt having the rig ready. "You just go on home to bed, Carlen. I'll take care of the mare and buggy."

He made his way down the plank walk and unlocked the front door and locked it back when he was inside. He hurried to the back door just in time to hear the three knocks. He unlocked the door and let Bill and Curtiss in and dropped the bar back in place. The living room of the apartment had one window with a blind and curtain so no one could see from the outside. He lighted the coal oil lamp and asked his friends to have a seat and he would build up the fire and make a quick pot of coffee before they laid out their plans.

Carlen placed cups on the kitchen table and filled them. He got his first look in the light at Bill Rose. He was a year older than Carlen's twenty six years. His hair and eyes were black showing that he might have some Indian blood in his veins. He would pass for a range rider anywhere he went. He carried a worn handle Colt in his holster and you could bet he knew how to use it.

"Bill, I need some help in the worst way. I'm tied here at the store and I want the people that I suspect are the ring leaders of the robberies and murder to think that I'm just an apron wearing store clerk. I need you to keep an eye on four men that live here in town. One of them has a ranch over in Utah, a rancher by the name of Grady Holmes. I think that he is the go between man that carries the orders to the men on his ranch for the job the four here in town have planned. "

Bill replied, "Carlen, I've been working for Pete Johnson for the last seven months just watching that ranch in Utah. I've seen Grady come and go from there several times. The next couple of days after he goes back to town his riders all leave together and I follow them as close as I can. I've watched them steal a few head of cattle from a few distant ranches and drive them across the border into Arizona Territory. Pete is only concerned if they try to steal another bunch of cattle from him. I've seen Grady come to the ranch with three other men. They seem to have a meeting and then I hear the next day that the bank here in town has been robbed."

"Bill, I bet you that the three men with Grady were Vernon Hull, Winfred Barnett and Giles Farnsworth."

"How did you know that, Carlen, were you watching the ranch too?"

"No, all four of the men are on the city council. They are the ones who sent a man to threaten the newspaper editor to change the mayor's offer for me to accept or reject. By the way, Bill, Pete told me that he had two riders that he did not trust, do you know them?"

"Yes, I know both of them and I don't blame Pete for not having any faith or trust in either of them. I think that they would back shoot a man just because they didn't have anything else to do. I wouldn't doubt they were not the ones who told the rustlers how easy it would be to rustle the last bunch from Pete. They were broke and it was two weeks until payday and they both came up with a pocket full of money. They claimed that they won it in a poker game at the Brown Mule Saloon."

"I need to tell you fellows something and it can go no farther than this room. The trip I made to Durango was to talk to the Federal Judge there. Judge Hayes read the letter that Curtiss sent him and then swore me in as a U.S. Marshal. He also gave me a power of attorney to swear in a deputy marshal if I needed to. Bill, if you will raise your right hand and repeat after me I'll hand you this badge. Then all of our undercover work will stand up in court against these crooks when we have the proof on them."

Bill asked, "Carlen, how can I explain this to Pete? I'm on his payroll as a spy and I can't just up and quit the old fellow without telling him the truth."

"You don't need to leave him, Bill. You don't tell him anything. You are doing the job he asked you to do only now you have the authority to arrest a person who is breaking the law. We can't let anyone know that we are marshals until we get absolute proof that the ones we arrest are the culprits who have been responsible for the crimes committed here. I suppose that you report to Pete ever so often don't you?"

"Yes, I come in at midnight every Monday night and give him a written report of what I've seen for the past week."

"Don't worry about taking Pete's money when he pays you. After we finish our job you can just give him back what he has paid you from now until we wrap this up."

Curtiss told them that he would report to Judge Hayes once a week on what progress that was made and their pay would be held in Durango until this was over with. "Bill, I will need a copy of what you give to Pete every week. I can send it without anyone thinking anything about it; I send mail two or three times a week to the court in Durango."

Bill Rose raised his right hand and repeated the oath and Carlen told him he was officially a U.S. Deputy Marshal. Carlen told him to keep the badge out of sight until he was ready to make an arrest.

They called it a night and Carlen let them out the back door and dropped the bar and went to bed.

Carlen slept an hour later than usual this Sunday morning. The café was closed for the day so he fixed his own breakfast of bacon, eggs and biscuits along with a fresh pot of coffee. He thought since this was his day off and the store was closed that he would attend Sunday service at the First Baptist Church. Services started at eleven o'clock so he had plenty of time to clean up the apartment and himself.

He left by the back door and stopped by the livery stable to check on his big dun horse. He then entered the church which was almost filled to capacity. A rancher and his wife scooted over and made room for him on the back bench. After the songs were over a tall thin preacher stood behind the pulpit and rendered the sermon to his congregation. The preacher, for all of his thinness had a voice that could keep you awake. He preached only for thirty minutes and his sermon was straight to the point. The song of invitation was sung by the choir and one of the elders said the dismissal prayer. The rancher extended his hand and said, "I'm Harvey Crowell and this is my wife Sara." Carlen shook the man's hand and told him his name and thanked the couple for sharing their seat with him.

"Sara and I have a ranch about four miles due south of town over in New Mexico Territory. If you should happen down our way stop in and visit with us."

Carlen told the man that he would but he worked for Farris Baker in his store and Sunday was the only day that he had off.

"Well, Carlen, if you tire out listening to my friend Farris, just come on down and I'll put you to punching cattle."

"I'll be sure and remember that, Harvey."

He went back to the store and changed into his range clothes, then saddled his horse and rode out to visit Pete Johnson.

Sunday was an off day at the ranch and most of his hands had gone into town.

"Climb off that good looking horse and come on in, Carlen. I was just telling the cook to fix me some lunch. I've been out checking on some bulls I bought a while back. I'll have him fix enough for both of us if you haven't eaten."

"I sure could eat a good lunch, Pete. The café in town is closed on Sunday and I'm not much of a cook."

Carlen told Pete of his meeting with Bill Rose. "Pete, I believe that you couldn't find a better man than Bill. He seems as solid as a granite boulder. He told me of his work for you and I told him to keep me posted. I told him if he could get a lead on anything that we could catch them in the act of any foul play I'll be there to help him."

"Bill is a man you can count on in any trouble that comes up. He wouldn't take a foreman's job of helping me run this ranch. He seems to like just being left alone to do things. He will never have any roots to settle down with. I guess you noticed that he has some Indian blood in him."

"I figured he might, but I won't hold that against him. It wasn't his doing that he was born that way. I figure it's what a man does and the way that he treats others is what really counts."

"I agree with you, Carlen, I just wish Bill would take a hold of a good job and settle down. I've known him ever since I moved up here from Texas and he hasn't changed one bit."

"Well, Pete, some people are like that. I have known men working stock that were top hands. They would just all of a sudden draw their wages and move on. Any one of them could have run a ranch better than the men they worked for. I guess they just want to see what's on the other side of the mountain."

"Carlen, I can tell that you're not like that. I wish you would come here and work for me. I will pay you better than Farris does and I sure need a good foreman. I'm getting on in years and I can't stay in the saddle much longer."

"Pete, as soon as we get this county rid of the trouble makers I'll try to make Farris understand that I'm just a cowhand at heart. I can't leave town until I can get proof that these four councilmen are the culprits that are behind all of it. Then I'll come out and we can talk it over then. I think the world of Farris, but I'll never make the grade as a store clerk."

They talked for a while longer, and then Carlen thanked him for the lunch, told the old rancher goodbye, and headed back to town.

Chapter Six

Carlen entered the back door of the store and put the heavy bar in place and made ready for bed. He looked forward to having lunch with Peggy tomorrow. He wondered how mad she would be at him when she found out that he was a lawman. Well, he has a job to do then it was back to being a cowboy. He hated to let Farris down but he just couldn't see wearing an apron the rest of his life when he could straddle a good horse and be out in the country where he felt he belonged.

The sound of breaking glass brought Carlen wide awake. He lay there for a minute listing for any other sounds. He then heard boot heels echoing on the wooden floor coming from the front of the building. He slipped out of bed and into his jeans and with his pistol in hand gently opened his door just a little. He could see a candle being lit across the hall in Farris's office. There were two men with a tow sack in one of their hands and the other pulling out three sticks of dynamite with a short fuse attached. He recognized the one holding the candle as the gunman that was with Vernon Hull in the café. He opened the door and told them to drop the dynamite and to raise their hands. The gunman dropped the candle and pulled his pistol and Carlen shot him. The other man raised his hands and said, "Please don't shoot me, I'm just being paid to blow the safe and I'm not armed."

He told the man to pick up the candle and light the lamp on the desk. Then lay down on your belly on the floor.

Carlen entered the office and saw that his shot had creased the gunman's head taking off part of the top of his ear. He picked up his gun and searched both of them to find a small pistol in the gunman's right boot. Knowing that the gunman would soon come around he tied both men's hands and feet. He moved the high explosives and placed them on top of the rollup desk and blew out the candle that had scorched the floor. The clock on the office wall chimed out four o'clock and Carlen knew that the first person to arrive would be Farris. Well, he just had a three hour wait unless Betsy or her dad saw the front window of the store broken out.

At six he heard Betsy call his name and he answered that all was okay and for her to send for her dad and Curtiss. Wilbur Jones climbed through the broken window and unlocked the front door. Curtiss arrived a few minutes later and asked Carlen what happened.

Carlen explained and asked him if he would get the mayor here quick. He needed some handcuffs and leg irons from the jail. He told him to stop by the doctor's office and ask him to look at the head of the wounded man he shot. The doctor arrived first and after cleaning and placing a bandage on the wound told Carlen that the man was just knocked out like he was hit with a hard punch. "He will come around and hurt for a few days but it's nothing to worry about."

Curtiss returned with the mayor and Carlen told him that he needed four pair of hand cuffs and two pair of leg irons from the locked up sheriff's office. The mayor gave Carlen a slight grin and told him he would get them, gladly. Carlen asked Curtiss if he would go to the stable and have the hostler saddle his horse and two more. "Ride my dun, Curtiss, and lead the other two to the back loading dock."

Farris arrived and was sick at the sight of his large window glass shattered. When he stepped into his office he was in for quite a surprise. The two men were tied and lying on his office floor with the wounded man moaning. He took one look at the top of his roll top desk and nearly fainted. "Carlen, are you alright? I hope this is not your blood on the floor."

"I'm okay, Farris, these two birds were just fixing to blow open your big safe when I persuaded them it was a bad idea. I'm going to have to take off from work for a few days if you don't mind."

"You just go right ahead, Son. I would too if I had been in your boots. I know how something like this can upset a man."

After the mayor had returned with the handcuffs and leg irons, the crowd left to get back to their daily routine. Carlen asked Farris to come into the apartment with him. "Farris, I'm going to have to take these two men to Durango and have them locked up in the jail there. I am going to file an attempted murder case on them and of an attempted armed robbery. I'm not the least bit upset or nervous. I just don't want anyone in town to know where I'm taking the men. I'm sure that the word will get out in an hour or so just as soon as the town wakes up."

"Can't you just lock them in jail here?"

"Who is going to watch over them and who is there to file charges too? They would be busted out of the jail tonight and we would have to go through something like this again. These outlaws have been caught red handed and I don't want them to go free and keep robbing and murdering people."

"You're right, Carlen. What can I do to help?"

"Just don't tell anyone where I'm taking them. If I don't get started now their friends will have time to catch me on the trail and kill me and turn them loose."

Curtiss helped Carlen get the men on the two horses and with them handcuffed with one pair, the other pair locked their hands to the saddle horn. The leg irons under the horses' belly would keep them from any escape. Carlen then looped a rope around each of their necks and told them if they tried to run that he would save the state from hanging them. He headed them down the alley way out of sight and toward the bend in the river. Instead of crossing the river he made them ride up the river for a couple of miles and head west toward the bench and Pete's ranch. He stopped a couple of miles from the house and dismounted the men one at a time and locked their leg irons around two large pine trees about twenty feet apart. They were in a dense part of the forest and could not be seen unless someone accidently stumbled upon them. It was noon time and the man with the headache caused by Carlen's shot was complaining about something to eat. Carlen told him if he didn't shut up that he would stick a piece of dynamite in his mouth and light the fuse. He quit his belly aching in a hurry.

Carlen waited until eleven o'clock that night and then saddled his dun and rode to Pete's house. Since this was Monday night he knew that Bill Rose would be here to give his report to Pete.

He tied his horse away from the house, walked quietly to the front porch and tapped lightly on the front door. Pete was dressed and was surprised to see it was Carlen. "I thought for sure that it would be Bill coming in to give me his report."

Carlen told him of the attempted robbery of Farris's big safe and that he had the two men locked to a couple of pine trees. ""Pete, I need Bill to go with me to Durango and get these two charged with robbery and attempted murder. I know that as soon as the town gets wind of their capture that their bosses will send some men out to kill me and release the prisoners."

"I can send ten men with you if you want me to."

"No, Pete, the less that's known about this the better chance we have to catch the big shots. I think that Bill and I can take a roundabout route and get them there safely without anyone knowing where they are."

"Well, I just don't want anything to happen to you, Carlen. You're the only one that has really got the ball rolling on trying to put a stop to this bunch of outlaws. I don't know how you're going to do it but I feel like you will finish up this mess and either kill them or have them put in jail for the rest of their lives. I'm sure glad they didn't get into Farris's safe because I've got quite a bit of money in it."

"Pete, I'm going to need some food to take along with us. We will also need a skillet, coffee pot and tin cups. I haven't eaten since we had that late lunch here yesterday afternoon. My prisoners are complaining about me not feeding them too. I left town just before sunup and didn't have time to put anything together."

"I can take care of that; come on into the kitchen and I'll get you filled up while we wait for Bill."

Pete fixed Carlen up with slices of honey smoked ham and thick slices of sourdough bread washed down with cold milk from his ice house. While he was eating Pete loaded down two flour sacks full of food and cooking utensils with four canteens.

Carlen heard the soft knock on the door and told Pete that Bill was here. Pete opened the door and Bill entered the kitchen and was surprised to see Carlen. Carlen told him of what happened in San Juan and that he needed him to help take the two culprits to jail in Durango.

"Partner, I'm ready to get them there and locked up. I'm happy that you have caught two of them in the act and maybe one of them will break down and confess to who they are working for."

Carlen told him the man he shot was one that he had seen in the café with Vernon Hull.

"I know of him, Carlen. He has supposed to have killed a few men in gun fights. I've seen him at the ranch owned by Grady Holmes over on the Utah border. From what I've heard about him he has served a few years in prison down in Santa Fe."

Pete placed a sandwich and a cold glass of milk in front of Bill and he wolfed it down and told Carlen he was ready to leave. The two shook hands with Pete and he wished them luck. Carlen told Pete if they made it Bill would come by and let him know of what the judge would do with the two outlaws.

Bill's mount was fresh and the other three were well rested. Carlen told Bill that they needed to be well away from Pete's range before daylight. "I think that we had better take a long way around instead of the regular trail to Durango. The first time I came up here I had to kill a man that took a shot at me and missed. I'm sure that they will have that trail covered in several places to ambush us."

"I know this country like the back of my hand, Carlen. We can ride a west circle over by Mesa Verde and catch the train in Mancos to Durango. It will take us a day longer but the trail is safe unless one or two of Pete's hands saw us leave. I don't think they did as we headed toward town when we left the ranch."

They aroused the two outlaws and with them bound and saddled they followed Bill as Carlen brought up the rear. With the ropes around their necks they knew better than to utter a word or Carlen would tighten the noose tighter. At good daylight they made a quick camp beside a small stream and Bill made a smokeless fire as Carlen loosed one side of the leg irons and unlocked the hand cuffs from the saddle horn. He helped the two men off and told them to sit on the ground and they would be fed and have a cup of coffee. Neither had a word to say as they quickly ate and the safecracker asked for another cup of coffee. Bill poured them each a cup as he and Carlen cleaned up the camp and put out the fire. Back in the saddle again they reached the south face of Mesa Verde at twilight. Bill led them to a spring with a small basin of water. He filled the canteens first and then the coffee pot before letting the four horses drink.

Carlen had chained the two men to two large juniper trees with their leg irons where they would eat and sleep. After the meal was finished Carlen handed the two men a bed roll each and told them they had better get some sleep as tomorrow would be a long day again.

 Carlen had a fire going as soon as it was light while Bill saddled the horses. Bacon with warmed over biscuits and coffee finished, the fire was put out and another day in the saddle began. Carlen marveled at the stone structures built under the huge overhanging cliff. He had never seen anything like it. Bill told him that the place was built by the Ancient Ones who first inhabited this part of the country.

They made it to Bud Wheeler's general store after dark and explained to him about the prisoners that they wanted to take to Durango on the train in the morning. Bud told them that there would be a night freighter in the station in about an hour and they could get tickets to ride in the caboose if they wanted to go on tonight.

"Mister Wheeler, can you stable our four mounts until we return for them?"

"Yes, I'll be glad to. I have a man cleaning out one stable now and I'll have him take good care of your mounts. You men sit down and I'll have my wife fix you some supper. By the time you finish the train should be here."

After they had finished, even the two outlaws told Mother Wheeler how good the meal was. Carlen paid the bill of fare and left a couple of silver dollars on the table.

Carlen explained to the brakeman of their prisoners and got his okay to ride in the caboose. Carlen paid him for the ride and in a few minutes the four were on the trip to Durango.

Bill knew where the sheriff's office was located and the two marshals had their prisoners locked in. They found a hotel room with a hot bath on each floor. After a bath and shave they crawled into bed for a good night's rest. Early the next morning the two men purchased some new clothes and left the dirty ones at the laundry. Carlen told Bill that it was a long walk to the Federal Building and maybe as early as it was they could see the judge before he started his daily routine.

The same lady asked them in and told them the judge should arrive soon. The chairs were a welcome seat after the long walk from the center of town. The judge arrived and shook hands with Carlen and then was introduced to Bill Rose. "You two men come on into my chambers and fill me in on what brings you here this morning."

Carlen explained to the judge of what had taken place at the attempted robbery and of him swearing in Bill as his deputy. "We have the two men locked in the jail here in Durango, as there is no way we could keep them in San Juan. One of the men has a slight head wound. He pulled his weapon on me and I creased his skull and the bullet took off part of his ear and knocked him out. I left the explosives at Bud Wheeler's store in Mancos. I know that it will be held for evidence at their trial, but I couldn't bring it here with these two prisoners along."

"Well, it looks like you two men are off to a good start on cleaning up this gang that is trying to get rich off the folks in San Juan County. I will have these two brought to my court for a hearing and will charge them both with attempted murder and robbery. I will set bail so high that the richest man in the state of Colorado can't post it. I'll set the trial date for next month and explain to each of them that their crime is punishable by hanging. Maybe this will get them to try to plea- bargain their way out of being hung. Do you two fellows need me to advance you some funds?"

"No, Your Honor, we can hold off until payday. I have had to rent the horses for the two men we have in jail ,but I will keep all of the receipts and turn them in when and if we get all of these crooks in jail."

"You men don't hesitate to wire me if I can be of any help. I'll write Curtiss when these two are set for trial. Carlen, you will have to testify since you were the one that made the arrest. You two need to be very careful and send me your weekly reports through Curtiss."The judge gave them each a firm handshake and told them again to be watchful.

The two marshals checked out of the hotel after the noon meal, picked up their laundry and caught the afternoon train to Mancos.

After a good supper cooked by Mother Wheeler they spent the night in a cabin that Bud Wheeler rented to wayfarers. Morning came and after a good breakfast they purchased a few supplies. Thanking the Wheelers and telling them goodbye they mounted up, leading the other two horses. They took the same trails back to San Juan.

Carlen told Bill that he would bypass Pete's ranch and enter town well after midnight to return the horses to the livery stable. "I had rather no one see me returning these rented mounts. I told Curtiss to tell the hostler not to say anything to anyone about the horses. The stable owner is a good friend of Farris and he doesn't like the town council at all."

"Carlen, I think I had better go back and watch the ranch Grady Holmes has over on the Utah border. I think that since the two men failed to loot Farris's safe they will try to steal some more of Pete's cattle. It seems like they have a schedule set up to try to rob or steal something every other week."

The two marshals departed company on the west boundary of Pete's ranch and Bill headed west and Carlen turned due south to enter San Juan from the west side of town. Carlen stabled the three horses and put the saddles and tack on the rail. He rubbed them down, gave each a generous feed of oats and filled their hay mangers without waking the hostler.

He took the alley to the back of the store and went to bed and was asleep almost instantly.

He was still sleeping when he heard the tinkle of the front door bell. He knew that Farris was getting ready to open for business. He quickly dressed and as Farris opened the door to his office he said, "Good morning boss."

Farris wasn't expecting Carlen to be back for a few more days and his greeting surprised him. Farris turned to face him and told him that he gave him a scare. "Carlen, my boy, you scared me out of a month's growth. I didn't think that you would be back this soon."

"I got in late last night and put up the horses without waking the hostler. I'm as hungry as a bear. If you haven't had breakfast I'll be happy to buy for both of us."

"No, I haven't; I just wanted to see if my safe was still here. Carlen, I don't know what I would have done if you hadn't been here to stop the two robbers."

"You won't have to worry about those two men ever again. Come on and let's see what Betsy has got for two hungry apron wearers."

Betsy said, "Well, Carlen, we thought that you had left town for good. After all of the shooting and the town people were chased out of the store, no one ever saw you again. Peggy came into town for lunch and was quite upset because you were to treat her to lunch last Monday. Curtiss treated her and I heard him say that maybe since she had that little pistol you were afraid that she might shoot you because you were still acting like a lawman."

Farris said to her, "Betsy, you had better be thankful that Carlen put a stop to them because a lot of folks, including Curtiss, keep their money in my safe since the bank was robbed."

Carlen had forgotten his promise to take Peggy to lunch. He figured that since he was involved in stopping the robbery that she would turn the cold shoulder to him and at the best she would become a distant friend.

The editor of the local weekly newspaper had made a hero of Carlen. Betsy showed him the paper and the front page blew up the story. The headline read LOCAL STORE CLERK SPOILS ROBBERS. Carlen told Betsy and Farris that he was going to have a talk with the editor.

Chapter Seven

September came and school started, along with it the first heavy frost of the coming winter. In a few days the leaves of the cottonwoods turned from a green to yellow shading, the oak brush leaves to a dull brown. In the higher elevations the quaking aspens were a bright gold. Red and crimson showed in the lower brush that grew on the mountain sides under the aspen. Late afternoons showed trails of smoke coming from the fireplaces. San Juan was preparing itself for old man winter. Every day coal bins were filled and wood piles split and stacked.

Farris had two large coal burning stoves for the store and two smaller ones for the office and apartment. Two weeks after Carlen had returned from Durango, Curtiss came by the store and asked him to come to his house after dark. Carlen gave him an okay nod and knew that Bill was in town with his weekly report and some news of what was going on at the ranch on the Utah border.

At closing time he told Farris that he was going to see Curtiss for a while before he had supper and would see him in the morning. He slipped on his ducking Texas brush jacket and took the long walk across the bridge to Curtiss's home. He had not seen or heard from Peggy since his return and prepared himself for the brush off he expected from her. Curtiss answered his knock and told him to come on in that Bill would be in after full dark. He didn't see Peggy so he figured that she was in her bedroom ignoring him.

Bill entered through the back door and shook their hands and told them that it was getting cold outside. "Well fellows, I have been staked out at the Utah ranch for the last two weeks and have seen a lot of activity coming and going. I watched a couple of crooked cattle buyers from Utah come by and have a meeting with all four of our town council members. I figure that they are getting ready to make a big steal from one of the large ranches in the area. I saw two men ride into New Mexico Territory in the direction of Harvey Crowell's ranch and come back from the same direction the next evening. Harvey runs a lot of cattle and he starts bunching them this time of year for the fall roundup. I figure that the rustlers will drive them down the river into Utah and let the buyer's crew pick them up there to drive on into Arizona Territory. By the time Harvey misses them they will be sold and butchered.

"I watched the two men that works for Pete make three trips to the Utah ranch and I have warned him of their dealings. He has put three of his best men to watch them to see if they are taking a few head of his stock and pushing it off of his range into the government land on his west boundary. If they are we won't have to worry about them anymore, Pete will hang them.

"I know that Harvey has a salty crew and I need you, Carlen, to ride over and warn him of what I think is going to happen. I've got to see Pete at midnight or I would go myself."

"I don't mind going at all, Bill. I met the man in church and he told me that his headquarters were only about four miles south of town. I'll saddle up and leave now. You take care and if you need me just have Pete send a rider and let me know where you are." The big dun horse needed a good workout so Carlen let him have his head for the first mile out of town then slowed him to a running walk. The lamp was still burning in the parlor of Harvey's home when he helloed the house. Harvey came to the door and told him to identify himself.

"Harvey, Its Carlen Ashton, I met you and your wife in church and I need to talk to you for a few minutes."

"Come on in, Carlen, and help me finish off this last pot of coffee."

Harvey Crowell was a very successful rancher. The home with it's beautiful furnishings would attest to that.

Carlen felt the friendliness of the rancher and his wife as she poured their coffee at the kitchen table.

"Harvey, I suppose that you know Bill Rose?"

"Yes, I sure do, he is a good man and a heck of a good cowboy."

"Well, he has asked me to come and visit you and to tell you of a possibility of a bunch of rustlers fixing to hit your herd pretty soon." He explained to the rancher of Bill spying for Pete Johnson and of the riders he had seen going and coming from toward his ranch. "Bill told me that you were the only large rancher in the direction that they traveled. He thinks that they will hit your cattle as they are being bunched for the fall round up."

"Carlen, I sure do appreciate you making this night ride down here to give me warning. I'll put some of my men on the north and west borders and see if we can't put a stop to some of this rustling. By the way, my wife and I want to thank you for keeping Farris's safe from being robbed. We never trusted the east coast banker so we just left our money with Farris when Hull opened his bank."

Carlen told them that he had better get back to town and thanked the couple for the coffee. It was after midnight when he stalled his horse and as he started to cross the street he felt the bullet hit him a second before he heard the sound of the pistol firing. The slug knocked him flat on his belly and he heard the hostler call out, "What's going on out there?"

He then heard someone running down the plank walk as the hostler saw him lying in the dusty street and came running to him. "Carlen, can you hear me? I'm going to get a lantern and see if I can get some help. I don't know how bad you're hurt but I'll be back as soon as I can."

Carlen vaguely remembered the next few hours. He felt hands moving him and could tell that he was being carried, and then he passed completely out. Next he felt as though he was being washed with warm water. When he opened his eyes the sun was creeping down the mountains west of town. He was in a white room with windows on three sides. He could smell the fresh clean air and could feel a slight chill in the room. He didn't hurt until he tried to sit up, then he remembered the shot. His left shoulder felt like it was twice as large as it should be. With his right hand he felt the bandages and then knew that he was in the doctor's home.

He heard the door open and the doctor stepped into the room. "Well, young man it looks like you have got your nap out. I guess that by now you feel like you could eat a bite. Am I correct?"

"Doctor, I feel like I could eat just about anything that had the hair taken off."

"My wife is fixing you up a good bowl of chicken soup. We can't let you have any solid food for a couple of days. You have got a big hole from your back to your chest just under your collar bone. A little lower and you wouldn't be here at all. It took a pretty good marksman to hit you shooting in the dark."

"I can't understand why anyone would try to kill me. I'm just a store clerk and the only enemies that I have are the two men who tried to rob Farris."

"My boy, when you put a stop to those two you made a lot of enemies in San Juan County. They were known outlaws to some of us and they have a lot of friends in this area, including people who think that they are of high esteem. I think that they are trying to rob, steal and murder their way to riches instead of working for it. They prey on the people who have worked all of their lives to have what they have."

"Well doctor, as soon as I get out of this bed I'm going to put on my pistol and see if I can't put a stop to it. There are too many good people here to have to put up with this bunch of outlaws. Anyone who would shoot a man in the back is a coward and I'm going to try to call a few of them out and see if they can stand up to a fair gun fight."

"Carlen, for everyone who will meet you in the street there will be two hidden to shoot you in the back again."

"I guess that is the chance I'll have to take doctor."

"Let's get you well first and then you will have a better chance to take them on."

Before dark Curtiss came to visit and told him that he didn't know that he had been shot until he stopped at the store to pick up a few things that Peggy needed. "Farris told me about it so I came on up here before going home. Do you have any idea who might have done this?"

"No, but I know who gave the order to have it done, and as soon as I'm well enough I'm going to make sure that he never gives an order to anyone else."

"Who do you think it is?"

"None other than Vernon Hull. I know that the man I shot in the store robbery is his right hand man. I've seen them together and Bill has seen them together at the Utah ranch. I also believe that Vernon robbed his own bank. Any other robber would have blown the safe. Farris told me that the robbers not only cleaned out all of the money but took all of the records and everything in the safe deposit boxes. No one but Hull would have done this. Those records mean a lot and the deeds to their property are all that a person has to prove that they owned the place except the recording of the deed in the county court-house. I bet if you look in the book of recordings that there are quite a few pages missing from the ledger."

"I never thought about that, Carlen. As soon as the county clerk's office opens in the morning I'll check and see how many pages are missing. I'd better get these things to Peggy and tell her of you being shot. I know that she will be here the first thing in the morning to visit you."

"Curtiss, I don't think she will. She seems to have a great dislike for ex- lawmen. "

"Well, she better change her mind or I'll change it for her."

"No, Curtiss, it won't work. Just let her make up her own mind."

"Anyway, I'll tell her of you being shot and where you are. I'll get word to Pete and Bill too."

Farris came by to visit him on his way home and asked if there was anything that he needed or could do for him.

"Farris, would you please bring me my pistol and shell belt as soon as you can? I have the feeling that since they didn't kill me they will try again. I also need to be moved to a room with no windows. If the doctor will let me I would like to be moved to the store. That way I would not endanger anyone here. I know that since I stopped the robbers from cleaning out your safe they won't rest until I'm dead. I guess that they think that I'm mad at them because I wouldn't take the job as sheriff with them appointing my own deputies."

"I'll talk to the doctor and see if we can move you to the store tonight. I'll hire a lady to be your nurse until you are able to take care of yourself."

"Farris, I think I can take care of myself now. I'll be okay as long as I don't open up the wound and get it started bleeding again. There is nothing wrong with my right hand and I can fend for myself. I can walk to the café to eat and can wash myself. I won't need to do anything else until these bullet holes scab over."

Farris explained to the doctor what Carlen wanted to do. He didn't like the idea of him getting out of bed so quick but agreed it would be better for all involved if he was in the apartment.

After dark the doctor and Farris hooked up the doctor's buggy and helped Carlen into the rear seat and took him through the back alley to the store. Once inside the building the doctor left him his medicine and instructed him how to take it. Farris helped him into bed and told him that he would bring him his breakfast as soon as Betsy opened the café. "Thanks, Farris, for taking care of me. I'll try to get my apron back on as soon as I can."

"Carlen, you don't need to even think about trying to come back to work. It's going to take you a long time to heal up and don't you try to push yourself."

He was awake when Farris brought him a heaping platter of eggs, bacon, fried crisp potatoes covered with cream gravy, three sourdough biscuits along with a cold glass of milk and a cup of steaming coffee. "Betsy must have known just how hungry I am, bless her heart. Thanks, Farris, for bringing me this great breakfast."

"Let me help you to the table, Carlen. I don't want you to fall and burst open that wound."

"Just stand close to me, Farris, so in case I should start to fall I can grab you with my right hand,"

Farris could see the pain as he slid to the edge of the bed and placed his feet on the floor. He sat there a minute and then slowly rose to his feet. He stood for a moment then walked to the kitchen table and eased into a chair. Sweat was breaking out on his forehead and Farris handed him a towel to wipe his face with. "Well, Farris, it wasn't easy but now I know that I can do it if I just take my time and watch what I'm doing."

"You eat up, Carlen, and if you need help getting back to bed just call me, okay."

"Don't worry, Farris, you and the whole town will probably hear me if I need you."

Farris left the room to get the store ready for the day and Carlen started putting the food away. He couldn't remember the last time he had a breakfast this good.

He took his time and made it back to bed without mishap and thought how good it was to have a friend like Farris Baker.

Around ten o'clock Curtiss came in and told him he went by the doctors and was really surprised that he had let him come to the store. "Peggy said that she would stop by to see you on her way to the schoolhouse, so I guess now that you're here she will stop by this afternoon. I went from the doctors to the court-house to look at the deed registration ledger and you were right about a bunch of missing pages.

"Since all of the property south of the river is in New Mexico Territory we won't have to worry about them as they are all in the record at Santa Fe. I couldn't find a deed to Farris's store, Pete's ranch, the local newspaper office and a bunch of others. You were right, Carlen, when you told us that these men wanted to own the whole county. I guess why they wanted to bust Farris's safe was to find those deeds to a lot of the properties that were not in the safe at the bank."

"Well, Curtis, all we have to do is find all of the missing ledger sheets and with them will be all of the money that Hull has stolen. I'm beginning to know where I think they may be."

After Curtiss left Carlen suddenly felt weak and really tired. The apartment door was closed and he could hear very little noise in the big store. Closing his eyes he fell into a deep sleep and Farris didn't awake him to see what he wanted for lunch. Late that afternoon he felt something warm in his right hand. He slowly opened his eyes and Peggy was sitting in a chair beside his bed holding his hand. She gave him a big smile and said, "Hello sleepy head."

Carlen returned the smile and gently squeezed her hand. "Farris told me that you slept through lunch so I told him that I would fix you something when you woke up. Just tell me what you want and I'll start cooking."

He looked at her and said, "You look like an angel, I could not ask for anything better than just to lie here and look at you."

"Carlen, you won't get well just looking at me. You really need to eat to build back up the blood that you have lost. You can look at me while I fix your supper. Now tell me what you would like to have."

"You just fix me whatever you think is best. I know that I owe you one lunch from the Monday I had to go to Durango. If you like we can walk to the café and I'll buy our supper."

"No. I will not see you up and around in the shape that you're in. The doctor told me that you were lucky to be alive. This is what you get for trying to act like a lawman. I'm going to cook your supper and I'll be here early in the morning before school time to fix your breakfast. So you just stay put and watch me fix your meal."

Looking at her with a grin he answered her, "Yes boss lady."

A week passed and Peggy was there every morning and afternoon. Saturday came and she spent the day helping him get his strength back. He told her that he felt like going to church in the morning if she would go with him in case he needed her help.

"I will be happy to go with you, Carlen. I think getting out in the fresh air and sunshine will help you mend faster. I'll come by at ten thirty and that will give us plenty of time for you to walk slowly. If the preacher gets longwinded we may have to get you back before service is over."

"Peggy, the hotel dining room will be open tomorrow and we can have dinner there after service is over."

She finished cleaning up the late supper dishes and gave him a peck of a kiss on the cheek and told him goodnight.

Carlen got up early Sunday morning and washed as best he could without using his left arm. He let it hang by his side instead of trying to wash with it. The doctor told him to keep it in the sling. He really felt good after shaving and getting dressed. He would do without breakfast knowing that the hotel luncheon would be enough. At twenty minutes after ten he hid his pistol in the sling and locked the front door of the store and sat on the bench under the porch covering the plank boardwalk. This was his first time to be outside since he was shot and he marveled how nature could change the country side so much in just a few days. He watched as Curtiss brought the buggy across the bridge and pulled up in front of the store. He left his seat and reached with his right hand to help Peggy down from the buggy.

Curtiss asked, "Carlen, we can take you in the buggy if you like?"

"Thanks, Curtiss, but I'd really rather walk and get some strength back in my legs."

"Okay, just take it easy. I'm going to pick up Betsy and we'll see you two at church."

Peggy took the right arm he offered her as they started in the direction of the white steeple on the roof of the church. He glanced down at her as she raised her face and smiled at him. "Carlen, I've got my doubts about you ever making the grade as store clerk. I know in my heart that you love the outdoors and the only way you'll be happy is to either be a lawman or a cowboy."

"Peggy, just between you and me before winter is over I'm going to be just another cowhand. I was raised on my parent's ranch in Texas and it's the best kind of life that a person could want. I have enough money saved to get a small spread and enough cattle to have a good start. I hope by then these thieves, murderers, rustlers and robbers are in the ground or in the state pen serving a life sentence."

"Carlen, please tell me that you are not going to be the one who has to put them there."

"Peggy, if I'm going to put my roots down in San Juan County I must do my part to help those who are trying to bring law and order back here. These people are trying to kill me because I spoiled their robbery of the big safe in Farris's store. If you only knew how many people are going to lose what they have worked for all of their lives I think that you would look at things very differently. They will take the store Farris owns, the Jones family café, Pete Johnson's ranch, the local newspaper, just to mention a few. This is an organized gang of criminals that someone's life means nothing to them. If a man has something they want they will get it by whatever means is necessary. Maybe you should sit down with Curtiss and he can explain the situation better than I can."

"Carlen, it's really hard for me to grasp people doing things like this. I guess that I've just never known that people could do things like this to others."

Harvey Crowell met them at the door of the church and Carlen introduced Peggy to him and his wife. "Miss Peggy, you have one of the best men I know as your escort. If it wasn't for him I would have lost a lot of cattle. Carlen, I want to thank you and Bill for letting me know what they planned for me. I heard about you being shot just a few minutes ago. I just want you to know that me and my men have made these rustlers pay an awful high price for trying to steal the herd. Let's get a seat before they are all taken up."

After service was over the couple took a slow walk to the hotel dining room and were seated at a table for two. After the meal was finished, they walked along on the plank walk when a man that was in between two buildings stepped in front of them. With his pistol he hit Carlen on his wounded shoulder and said, "Lawman, if you have a prayer to say you better start now and make it a short one for I'm fixing to put a bullet in your head."

Without thinking Peggy pulled the double barrel derringer from her purse and fired two shots into the man. He fell backwards on the plank walk as dead as a man can get. The shots brought a crowd from the hotel and the Brown Mule Saloon. Carlen thought that Peggy would go into hysterics but she was as calm as could be and explained to the crowd what had taken place.

Carlen had removed his coat and blood was seeping through his shirt and sweat was running down his cheeks. The mayor was in the crowd and told a man to help get the couple in his buggy and he would take them to the doctor. When they entered the doctor said, "Carlen, I can't believe you went to church and got shot again in the same place." Peggy explained to the doctor what had happened as the doctor removed the bloody shirt and removed the bandage.

After cleaning and dressing the wound he told them that there would be a large bruise where he was hit with the pistol. "Well, Carlen, It's not too bad of an injury. You will just take a little more time to heal. As long as you keep taking care of it like you have been you'll be just fine."

Curtiss and Betsy had found out what happened and were on the porch waiting for the doctor to release him. When they came out Peggy had to tell again of what happened. They helped Carlen into the back seat of the buggy and Peggy held on to his right arm. When they arrived at the store, Harvey and his wife along with Farris and Pete were waiting for them. Again Peggy had to tell them what happened. They got Carlen in bed and Pete told Farris that he was going to send two of his men down to sit in the store day and night to make sure that no one tried again to kill Carlen or break open the big safe. The town undertaker came in and told them that he found a wanted poster on the dead man. He had killed a banker in Garden City, Kansas and the reward was for one thousand dollars dead or alive. He gave the poster and the papers he found on the man proving his identity to Curtiss. He handed him ten new twenty dollar gold eagles that was in the man's pocket telling Curtiss it was blood money someone paid to have Carlen killed.

When the couple were alone Peggy asked, "Carlen, who is Bill and what is this warning Harvey Crowell all about?"

"Bill Rose is a man that works for Pete Johnson. He is what we in the west call a stray man. He watches to see if someone is trying to steal a ranchers cattle and drive straying cattle back home. Bill was watching two rustlers and they were looking to steal a bunch of Harvey's cattle. Bill asked me if I would go to Harvey's ranch and warn him of what was fixing to happen. I rode down there and told him of the rustler's intent. That was the night that I got shot just after I put my horse in the stable. From what Harvey told us at church he must have been successful at stopping the rustlers."

Suddenly Peggy placed her head on Carlen's right shoulder and put her arms around his waist and started shaking and crying. He put his right arm around her and held her tightly against him until the shaking and crying stopped. They sat together on the edge of the bed and Peggy said, "I can't believe that I just, without thinking, killed a man. The man I shot was the man that has been following me ever since I arrived here. When he hit you with that big pistol all I could think of was to shoot him."

"Peggy, you saved both of our lives. I had my pistol hidden in the arm sling but when he hit me it seemed to paralyze my entire body. I tried to reach for the gun but my body wouldn't obey my brain. I'm thankful that you did what I couldn't do."

She stayed the rest of the afternoon. She then cooked their supper and as she was washing the dishes there was the tinkle of the bell. Farris and two men with him came in and Farris told them that these were the two cowboys that Pete had sent down to keep Carlen company in case he had any more visitors. Peggy told them goodnight and let Farris take her home in his buggy.

Chapter Eight

Two weeks went by and it seemed that a quiet peace had settled over the town of San Juan. The two riders that Pete had sent were great company to Carlen as he grew stronger each day. Peggy came by with Curtiss every evening and they had supper together with Betsy in the café.

Another week passed and Curtiss brought news that the judge in Durango had set the trial date for the next Thursday and for Carlen to appear as his witness. "Carlen, there is a weekly stage that comes through here and goes to Shiprock and stops in Mancos by way of Cortez. It's a three day trip to Mancos but I think it would be better on you than riding a horse. The stage stops at night and you can sleep in a hotel rather than on the ground. The stage leaves in the morning and that will give you a day's rest in Durango before you have to appear in court."

"I think that would be the best, Curtiss. I don't feel exactly like a three day horse ride right now. I was hoping that the judge would get one of the outlaws to plea-bargain for a lighter sentence."

"Carlen, if the judge does what I think he will do, then I think that one of them will speak up rather than being hung. I'm sure that they both will get the death penalty."

Carlen was at the hotel in the early morning darkness when the stage driver called for him to climb aboard. He was the only passenger so he set his valise in the floor of the stage. He had on a sheepskin coat to ward off the morning chill. His pistol was in the holster of the shell belt covered by the long coat. The sway and bounce of the coach never stopped. His big dun horse would have been a lot more comfortable. The mountain road took its toll on the four horse hitch and the driver would stop at the crest of the hills to let them get their wind. Carlen decided that the driver's seat would be more comfortable with less dust than inside the coach. When the driver pulled up for the next stop Carlen got out and told the driver that he would like to sit with him. "Just crawl on up here cowboy as I could use some company."

By the time they made the first nights stop Carlen was well versed on the life and times of a stage driver.

The stage finally pulled into Mancos and Carlen bid the driver goodbye and with his valise in hand walked over to the Wheeler store. Bud was standing on the porch and stuck out his hand and said, "Welcome back, Carlen, it's good to see you again. Come on in and I'll tell my wife that we have a friend that's ready for a good supper."

"Bud, for the last three days I had wished that the stage had wings and could fly. I've had some of the worst food that could be cooked on this trip. I think I could eat Mother Wheeler's frying pan and it would taste better than what I've been fed."

"Carlen, we heard about you getting shot and about Curtiss's sister shooting the other man that tried to kill you. I am beginning to think that you are the most unpopular man in San Juan."

"Well, Bud, there are a few people down there that must think the world would be better off if I just disappeared."

"Carlen, the world would be a whole lot better off if those who want you dead were burning in the devil's roasting pot."

"That's what I've got to go to Durango for is to testify against those two that Bill Rose and I took to jail. I hope that the judge puts them away for a long time."

"Carlen, I know the judge real well, and he won't fool around with these kinds of men. I'll bet you ten dollars to a doughnut that he sends them both to the gallows."

"I sure do hope he does; I caught them red handed fixing to blow up Farris's big safe. The one who pulled a gun on me has spent time in the Santa Fe prison. Bill told me he was as bad as they get."

Carlen spent the night in the little cabin and caught the early morning train to Durango. He took a room in the three story brick hotel and had his bath and shaved. He had lunch at the Cattleman's Steak House and purchased a change of clothes. The more he saw of the town of Durango the better he liked it. The people were friendly and the town was clean as a whistle.

The Animas was a clear swift running river that wound its way through town. This town would not be like the cow-towns that he had seen live for a few years and then seem to be blown away by a dust storm. Durango was here to stay. If a person could live on the beautiful scenery they could live here without working. He looked around town then went back to the hotel and rested until supper.

The narrow gauge train whistle woke him up the next morning just as it was getting good daylight. He washed his face, combed his hair and was ready for a good cup of hot coffee. There was a café open a block north of the hotel and their breakfast special was too good to turn down.

He knew that the judge would want to talk to him before court was in session so he got his early morning exercise walking. He was glad that he had worn his sheepskin lined coat. The breath of everything was frosting as the warm breaths collided with the early morning air.

The lady with the tight rolled bun in her hair let him in and told him to go on into the judge's chambers. The judge's door was open and he rose from behind his desk and shook hands with Carlen and told him to take a seat. "Carlen, I heard a few things of your trouble and I hope you are now doing well."

"Yes, Your Honor, I'm doing fine. I'm still a little sore but that's to be expected."

"Well, court will convene at nine this morning and I wanted to bring you up to date on our prisoners. The man you shot is a wanted felon in New Mexico Territory. With his past record he will hang. The other man has served three terms in prison for robbery and safe cracking. I'm going to try to hang him also. He will crack when he knows that he is going to hang. This can be the best chance that we have had to implicate one or more of the four men who head up this gang of outlaws."

"Judge, I spent the night at Bud Wheelers and brought the dynamite with me to use as evidence." He placed the three sticks with the short fuse on the desk. "Don't get careless, Judge, and light your pipe with this stuff on your desk."

"I'll have my bailiff remove the fuse and cap so it will lessen the danger in the court room. Carlen, the defense attorney is trying to make a name for himself so don't let him get you confused. He will try every trick in the book to try to get you to make a mistake."

"Your Honor, all I'm going to do is tell the truth. He can badger me all he wants to but he will just waste the court's time."

"Well, I'd better get my robe on and get ready for the day. I'll see you after we get these men back behind bars."

Carlen went to the restroom first then seated himself in the courtroom. The two attorneys were at their assigned tables and the sheriff and two deputies brought the two felons in and seated them. In a few minutes the bailiff called the court to order and asked the people to rise as he called Judge R.L. Hayes presiding. The judge didn't fool around. He asked the defense if he was ready and then the prosecutor, both answered, yes Your Honor. He told the sheriff to remove the last man to be tried from the court room. The two deputies took the safecracker to the holding cell and the prosecutor stated the charges on the gunman. Carlen was called to the stand and sworn in. He told the court exactly what happened. The witness was then passed to the defense. Carlen answered each question with a yes or no. the Judge was right about the hardnosed lawyer. The man tried every way he knew to cross Carlen up but to no avail.

The two outlaws chose not to have a jury trial; they knew that they wouldn't have a chance with their records in front of twelve men who were cattlemen and town merchants.

The two attorneys rested their case and the judge ordered the accused to stand. The man gave Carlen a hard look as he rose to his feet. The judge pulled no punches, death by hanging the first Monday of next month.

The safecracker was brought in and the process was repeated. After the testimonies were given and the attorneys rested their case, the same hanging sentence was given to the safecracker. The defense attorney threw a fit. "You can't hang a man for attempting to crack a safe, Judge."

The judge reached in his desk drawer and pitched the three sticks of dynamite to the lawyer who fled the court-room.

The safecracker pleaded with the judge not to hang him. "If you will cooperate with the court, and involve the people who paid you to do this robbery, I would consider sparing your life. Otherwise you will hang just the same as your friend."

"Judge, if I squealed on him my life wouldn't be worth a plug nickel."

"You are going to hang by the neck until you're dead the first Monday of next month so all you have to bargain with is your own life. Think it over."

The judge adjourned his court and they all rose as he left the room.

The sheriff escorted the safecracker back to the jail and Carlen sat in the empty court room. A minute after the sheriff had closed the door the judge opened the door from his chambers and motioned for him to join him.

"Carlen, before that man hangs he will give me a sworn statement telling us the name and or names of the masterminds. When I have the statement, I will send you an arrest warrant for whoever they are. You can put on your badge and you and Bill Rose can arrest them."

"Judge, I will need a search warrant to search the Brown Mule Saloon owned by Winfred Barnett, also one for his residence, another for the ranch and residence of Grady Holmes, another for the residence and office of Giles Farnsworth.

"I believe that the safecracker will name Vernon Hull as the one who paid him and the other man to blow up the safe. I will need a search warrant for him also."

"Carlen, if these other men are not named why need a search warrant for them?"

"Judge, when the bank was robbed I know that Vernon Hull robbed his own bank. There was no damage of any kind. All of the safety deposit boxes were opened and all records of deposits and bank balance sheets were taken. There were several deeds to a lot of property taken. The ledger sheets in the county clerk's office are missing that match the ones taken from the bank. If I can't find them a lot of people can't prove what they own. I am almost sure that these papers and the money are in the safe at the saloon or in one of the others men's possession. I need to find these things when I arrest Hull or I may never find them."

"I completely agree with you, Carlen. I had no idea that this was taking place in San Juan. Do you think that you will need me to send to Denver for more marshals to assist you?"

"No, Sir, Bill Rose and I can call on Pete Johnson and he has some very trustworthy riders should we need them. Pete has been keeping an eye on these outlaws for a long time. Bill was working for him when I asked him to become a marshal. I think that it would be for the best to let the people in San Juan help me if it becomes necessary."

"Carlen, I am thankful that you have risked your life and have given myself and the people of San Juan your services. The decisions are yours.

I'll have you a copy of the sworn statement and all of the warrants in your hands as soon as I have the man's confession."

"One more thing, Judge. Please be careful throwing that dynamite around as it can explode without the fuse or the cap."

"Really, are you sure?"

"Yes, Sir. I'm positive."

Carlen caught the up bound freight to Mancos and was ready for Mother Wheeler's good cooking.

Chapter Nine

    The stage wouldn't be there to pick up south bound passengers for three more days. Carlen rented a good horse from Bud and Bud stuck a 45/70 Winchester in the rifle boot and handed Carlen a box of shells and told him to keep it as long as he needed it. Carlen shook the store owners hand and thanked him. Mother Wheeler came running from the store with a flour sack stuffed with good eats and patted him on the arm and told him to take care.

    The bay horse was a good one and Bud had a bedroll and slicker tied on the back of the saddle. He made his first night's camp at the same spring where he and Bill had camped with the two prisoners. The next morning was cloudy and not a breath of air was stirring a leaf on any tree. The bay horse was stamping his hooves and was ready to go. The day seemed to get darker as he rode southeast. He stopped at noon to give his mount a breather and have a sandwich washed down with spring water. Around three o'clock he felt a snowflake touch his right cheek. It wasn't but just a few minutes until the bottom seemed to fall out of the clouds and fill the air with snow so thick that he couldn't see fifty feet in front of him. He knew that he should find shelter for himself and his horse as quickly as he could. The trail crossed a wide ravine and instead of crossing it he reined the horse down the ravine headed toward the southwest. The farther he rode the deeper the ravine became and was getting narrower. He spotted an overhanging rock bluff that extended twenty feet or so into the ravine wall. He dismounted and led the bay under the overhang. The bay stood without tying or being hobbled. He was a well trained horse. He unsaddled and rubbed him down with the saddle blanket and then started gathering fire wood. The bed of the ravine was littered with dead wood washed down from the mountains. At least he knew that he wouldn't freeze to death. It wasn't much below freezing but he knew that if the wind started blowing hard the temperature would drop like a rock.

    He could stand up almost to the back of the overhang so he led the bay as far as he could get him and built a fire about in the center of the shelter. He knew that he needed to stack in as much wood as he could before darkness set in. It was growing darker by the minute and the snow was still falling heavily. Well, all he could do was just wait the storm out. He fixed a pot of coffee and had a piece of Mother Wheeler's mince meat pie and called it supper. Placing the slicker on the sandy floor he placed his bedroll on it and set there to watch darkness engulf the world. Sleep he knew would be a long time in coming so he just relaxed and enjoyed the silence and his coffee. As he watched the veil of snow at the mouth of the overhang reflecting the fire light, he felt the bay horse nuzzle his back. The horse loved the company of a man. Carlen got up and patted the bay and talked to him as he would a person. He made up his mind that if Bud Wheeler would sell him this horse he was going to buy him. He loved his big dun but a man can always use two good horses.

He finally fell asleep around midnight after placing a large log on the fire. Daylight came with a bright sun glaring into the face of the overhang. Carlen rolled up his bedding in the slicker and stirred up the fire and had a cold biscuit with a warmed over cup of coffee. He gave the bay a biscuit and rinsed out his coffee pot and saddled up. The morning was cold but there was not a cloud in the sky as he rode out of the ravine. The bay was ready to travel and Carlen gave him his head as the horse stepped easily through the foot of snow. One more cold night on the trail and he spent the next one in Pete Johnson's bunk house with his riders. He had breakfast in Pete's kitchen and told him of the two men being sentenced to hang.

"Well, Carlen, me and my riders hung the two men that I told you I didn't trust. We caught them pushing about fifty head of my steers onto the federal land for the Utah rustlers to pick up, so we gave them a trial that was just as fair as if it was done in the courthouse. They admitted that they were guilty so we saw that justice was done."

"Well, Pete, that makes six of them that won't commit anymore crimes. I just hope that we can get the big shots of this bunch swinging on a rope pretty soon."

He thanked Pete for the bunkhouse bed and the breakfast. He told him he needed to get back and see if Farris had fired him yet.

"If Farris is that dumb, you just ride back up here and go to work for me."

"You can count on it if he has."

Carlen rode into San Juan before lunch time and stabled the bay horse next to his big dun. He brushed the bay down and gave him an extra quart of oats and a manger full of hay. He walked to the store and found Farris dusting the shelves in the women's department. "It's good to have you back, Carlen. I didn't look for you back until next week when the stage comes in."

"If I hadn't rented a horse from Bud Wheeler, I would have been on the stage. I just couldn't sit and wait three days to ride that stage again. I knew that you needed some help so I tried to get back as soon as I could."

"Tell me what the judge did to the two who tried to bust my safe open."

"He sentenced both of them to hang the first day of next month."

"Well, that is a harsh sentence but I guess they both deserved it. At least we don't have to worry about them trying it again."

"Farris, it's almost lunch time, why don't you go on and eat and I'll handle the store for you."

"I'm really kind of hungry. I've worried about you being off by yourself. I guess you got caught in that quick snow storm."

"It wasn't that bad. I found a good shelter for me and my mount and never had a problem. You go on and eat I'll hold the fort down while you're gone."

Farris placed his apron under the counter and told him he would be back as quickly as he could.

"Take your time boss or you will wind up with indigestion."

Curtiss Fletcher tinkled the door bell and said, "Carlen, we didn't expect you back until next week. I guess that a horseback ride home was better than the stage."

"You bet it was, and trail food is better than anything they serve at the way stations. I rented a horse from Bud Wheeler and Mother Wheeler fixed me up with a sack of her good cooking."

"I suppose that the judge sentenced both men to the gallows didn't he?"

"He did, and it didn't take him long to get it done. He told me that the safecracker would give him a sworn statement before he hangs. Then Bill and I can start arresting and searching for the missing ledger papers, deeds, and money taken from the bank. Things may get a little mean when we start serving all of the warrants I asked the judge for. He will send all of the paper work to you and then we can go to work."

"Carlen, that's going to be a rough job for just you and Bill. Didn't the judge offer to send you some help?"

"Yes, he did, but I told him that I could rely on Pete Johnson and a couple of his riders. I had rather the people of San Juan County be involved in cleaning up this bunch. Pete and his men know most of the men we're going after and also know the country in case we have a running fight on our hands. The judge agreed and told me to handle it my own way. All we are waiting for is the sworn statement from the safecracker and the arrest and search warrants.

"Curtiss, how is Peggy doing? After shooting that man that was fixing to shoot me I knew that she would have a hard time."

"Farris, Pete Johnson and I had a long talk with her while you were gone to Durango. I think since we three told her of how it was out here in the west and of the type people we are having this trouble with that she has a good understanding of things. She seems to have gotten a hold of herself and is the same self reliant sister that I have always known."

"I just hope that she will understand that I'm not doing this just because I was an officer of the law before I met her. Someone has to help the people here get their town and county back. I just happened to get involved and can't seem to stop until it's finished."

"Carlen, you are a blessing to the people of San Juan County. If you hadn't come along Farris's safe would be empty of all of the deeds and money from this county. These people owe you a lot of thanks not only for that but for how you have taken hold to rid the county of this bunch of outlaws and murderers."

"Curtiss, I just hope that we can get this over with without having some of our people killed. Anytime a gang like this bunch is being arrested and their little empire is coming apart there is always bloodshed on both sides. That's what worries me the most."

"Carlen, in every war that has been fought there is always that chance. Let's just hope that the only deaths that occur are not on the side of the people who are fighting for their rights and justice."

Farris returned from lunch and told Carlen to go eat. Carlen asked Curtiss if he wanted to go with him, but he had already eaten. He seated himself at the same table close to the kitchen. Betsy said with a smile, "It's good to see you back home, Carlen. Farris told me you were minding the store for him. He told me of the sentence the judge gave the robbers. Maybe this will put an end to all of the trouble."

"I'm afraid that this is just the beginning, Betsy."

"Well, I've seen a lot more men that work for Grady Holmes in the last few days. I thought that they were leaving the country."

"I sure wish they were, Betsy, but I don't think that is going to happen. I think that they are getting ready to really get mean since six of their buddies have been disposed of."

"What is it that they want, Carlen?"

"The town and the county all wrapped up in a neat package without paying the folks here a single penny. They have rustled and sold enough cattle to have built enough cash reserve to pay the outlaws that work for them. With the funds, deeds and records taken from the bank all they need now is what's in the big safe in Farris's office. When they get that then the town and county will be theirs."

"How can that be possible? My parents own this café and do not owe a penny on it or our home. They can't just tell us to pack up and leave all that we have worked for."

"Betsy, your deeds and the recording of them in the ledger in the county clerk's office do not exist. They have been stolen by this bunch of thieves. You cannot prove that you have ever owned them. To fight the battle in court will be very expensive and will be drawn out for years. The only way to stop it is get all of them in jail or dead with proof that they have stolen these deeds and recorded sheets. I'm asking you to keep this under your hat and not to even let on that you know about anything that I've told you. Curtiss, Bill Rose and I are working undercover to see if we can't put a sudden stop to their plans. Pete Johnson and his riders are going to be in on the fight too when it occurs. Just remain calm and don't speak a word of this to anyone except Curtiss."

"Carlen, you don't worry about me saying anything to anyone. I never thought that something like stealing a county could ever happen. I hope you fellows get every one of them in jail or the cemetery."

Pete Johnson came in and joined Carlen and ordered lunch. "Well, Carlen, what's our next step?"

"Pete, I think that you need to keep two men day and night in the store with two men in the back of the store and two in front. Betsy just told me that she has seen a lot of men that works for Grady Holmes come into town the last few days. I think that they will try to bust the safe in Farris's office at anytime or try to steal it, loading it on a wagon and getting it out of town in the dark of night when everyone is sleeping. I may be wrong but I think that they are getting desperate to have the rest of the deeds and the money that's in the safe. We have killed four of their men and two are in jail. I figure that they know that we are planning to roust them out pretty soon and they need what's in that safe before we do.

"I wish that the judge would hurry up and get the paper work to Curtiss so we could get a jump on them. If they get the contents of that safe we are in for a long hard fight in court."

"We could just forget about the law, Carlen, and just hang them now."

"Pete, we would then be classed as people who are as bad as they are. I feel like taking a gun and just shooting the whole mess of them but if I killed just one person that was not guilty I would be a murderer. I knew of some fellows that hung a man for stealing cattle and they found out the next day that the man wasn't guilty. One of them told me that it was something that bore a hole in his conscious every minute of his life."

"I know that you're right, but it makes me feel like I'm leaving the gate open and all of the things that the good people here worked so hard for is just running out the open gate."

"Well, let's just keep an eye on Farris's safe until the judge sends the orders to proceed. If we catch them in the act of trying to blow it open or steal it then we can do what has to be done without the papers."

Pete stationed his six men for the daylight shift and replaced them with six more for the night shift. These men had worked for Pete several years and had fought Indians and rustlers and weren't afraid to shoot when they knew what to shoot at and when to pull the trigger. For four nights Carlen got a goodnight's sleep in his apartment. On the fifth night in the wee hours of the morning he was awakened at the sound of a blast that shook the building, then the sound of pistols and rifles. He heard a wagon racing down the alley behind the building and a wounded horse screaming. Ten minutes later lanterns were lighted and he could see the big double doors of the loading dock were blown off. Pete's riders were looking to make sure that several men on the ground were dead. Carlen called out that he was coming out of the store so they wouldn't mistake him for one of the robbers. He counted six men dead and two wounded with the lead horse of a four horse hitch up dead in the harness. The other three were standing as the dead one stopped any movement of the wagon. There was a two wheel hand cart in the bed of the wagon. Carlen knew that the men planned to roll the big safe to the loading dock and place it in the wagon.

The blast of the dynamite to blow off the doors and the gunfire that followed woke up a lot of the town folks who had come to see what was happening. The doctor arrived and was looking to see how bad the two wounded men were hurt. The two of Pete's men stationed in the store as well as the two who were hidden in the alleyway were unharmed. The doctor told Carlen that the two wounded men would die before daylight.

When Farris arrived he couldn't believe what had happened to his store. The first thing he wanted to know was if Carlen was hurt from the dynamite blast. "No, Farris, I was asleep when the doors were blown off and the shooting started. Pete's men took care of all of the robbers without my help. We need to get some carpenters here to get a new set of doors built and the back frame work repaired before dark. It's going to be mighty cold in the store with the north wind blowing in."

"Well, let's have our breakfast while Pete's riders are watching things. I will go then to the lumber yard and get their crew up here and get started on the repairs."

The café was almost full by the time Farris and Carlen had finished their meal. Farris was asked so many questions that Carlen slipped out after paying Betsy and leaving her a tip.

Peggy stopped by on her way to the school house and was shocked by the devastation caused by the blast. Carlen was thankful that all of the bodies had been taken away by the local undertaker and the dead horse along with the wagon removed.

"Carlen, did you shoot any of the men who did this?"

"No, I was asleep when the blast woke me up. I never fired a shot or saw any of Pete's men shoot at anyone. I know that some of the robbers were shot but I didn't know who was wounded or who was killed."

"Do you think that this will put an end to all of this violence?"

"No, I do not. I think this is the beginning of the end. Soon there will be some U.S. Marshals here that will put an end to this gang who are trying to steal the town of San Juan and the county. There will most likely be bloodshed and more deaths before this town has any real peace. If they had gotten away with Farris's safe last night the people here would have really taken to killing everyone whom they thought was ever connected with this bunch of crooks."

"I really don't understand what this is all about. I guess you or Curtiss will explain things to me when this is all over."

"Peggy, just as soon as it's finished I'm going to be a cowboy and a rancher, and if you will let me take you to the dance I promise not to step on your toes."

"I just hope that you are not involved in all of this getting rid of this band of outlaws. I don't want to see you shot again. I hate myself for killing that man that was going to kill you. I don't think I could do it again even if the person was threatening to kill me."

"Peggy, there is no way that I cannot stay out of being involved. What I am fixing to tell you now must not be known by anyone else. If you breathe a word of it to anyone I'll be dead before sundown."

"What are you trying to tell me, Carlen? I promise that I will not say a word to anyone. I just hope and pray that you're not going to be involved in another gun battle."

"I hope that no weapons will be fired by either side, but the first shot will have to be fired by the outlaws. Peggy, I am a U.S. Marshal and it's my responsibility to see this county free from these men who are trying to steal everything these people in San Juan County own. I intend to live the rest of my life here and I want to live in peace and be able to look the people in this town in the eye and have them show respect for me as I have for them. I can't turn my back on you or anyone else here. I'm here to do a job that I have sworn an oath to do and I'll do it or die trying."

"I guess I knew it in my heart all along, Carlen. I knew when you removed your hat and bowed to me that first day I was in Farris's store that you were someone special. I wanted so much for you to escort me to the dance that I made myself ask you. You're very special to me, Carlen. I would just die if anything happened to you. I understand your duties to yourself and the oath that you have taken because that is the kind of man you are. I know that you will lay down your life for the people you are sworn to protect. Promise me that when you complete your mission here that you will belong to me and not the badge for the rest of your life."

He put his arms around her and promised that when this was finished he would take her for his wife and nothing else would ever come between them again. She, with watery eyes, kissed him and told him that she loved him more than life itself.

Chapter Ten

The first day of the month came and there was no word from the judge. Carlen was starting to have the thoughts that the safecracker wouldn't give the judge the information they needed and was going to the gallows with his partner. On the sixth day of the month a rider came into the store and asked for the location of the home of Curtiss Fletcher. Farris gave the man directions to his office and home and told him that Curtiss would be in his office now and he could catch him there. The rider thanked Farris and rode to the office.

The man entered Curtiss's office and deposited four sealed envelopes on his desk and said, "The judge asked me to give these only to you. If you will sign that you have received them I'll head back to Durango."

Curtiss signed the paper and thanked the rider and told him to tell the judge thanks for his efforts to help the people in San Juan.

 Curtiss opened each envelope and each contained the warrants to search the homes and businesses of the four men in question. Only one arrest warrant was in the envelope which was for the banker, Vernon Hull. Included with it was a copy of the sworn statement from the safecracker naming Hull as the man who paid them to rob the safe in Farris's store and to kill anyone who tried to stop them.

There was a light snow falling as Curtiss made his way to the San Juan Emporium store to give the warrants to Carlen. He dreaded the burden and danger that these warrants would place on Carlen and Bill Rose. Well, he told himself to just get a weapon and help them. My sister did it so why can't I? He knew that Pete Johnson and his riders would give the two marshals all of the help they probably needed, but he felt that he should also.

The large store was void of customers. Farris and Carlen were busy stocking the shelves with new merchandise from the large storeroom in the basement of the building. The coal fired heaters had the large store warm and the different odors of all of the different items in the store filled the air with smells that aroused ones senses.

At the tinkle of the bell Farris said, "Well, what are you up to this snowy morning, Curtiss? I guess that you got tired of looking at the start of old man winter and decided that it was time to bless us apron wearing clerks with your presence."

"I wish that my visit was only that, Farris, but I have what Carlen has been waiting for from the judge in Durango. I now fear for him and Bill and the others who help them with the task that lies before them."

"Well, let's just have a chair over by the heater and see what we need to do about this trouble that you have in your hands."

After they were seated Curtiss handed the envelopes to Carlen. He opened the one for Vernon Hull first and read it carefully and said, "Well this is just what I expected. Hull is where we will start, he is the only person named as the one who ordered the safe to be robbed and to kill anyone who interfered."

Carlen stood up and removed his apron and told Farris that he could no longer be a clerk for him. He folded the apron and placed it under the counter and told them that he had to find Bill Rose.

"What do you mean that you can't clerk for me any longer?"

"Farris, I'm going to let Curtiss fill you in on all of the facts. I've got to find Bill and get started as soon as we can. He went to the apartment and in a few minutes returned with his bedroll, slicker, and the 45/70 Winchester. He had on his sheepskin lined coat and his Texas Stetson.

"Curtiss, you and Farris keep a look out for Hull. As soon as I find Bill I need to catch Hull in the Brown Mule Saloon. If you see him ride out of town just watch the direction he leaves in. I'll get back as soon as I find Bill."

Carlen saddled the bay gelding and put a halter with a lead rope on the big dun. He slid the rifle in the boot and told the hostler he didn't know when he would be back. He paid him his stable bill in full. When he mounted the bay the hostler placed his hand on the horse's neck and said, "Carlen, I've got a feeling that this town is fixing to break wide open in a few days. I've had more of hard looking men coming in and out of this livery stable than there ever has been. I've heard Grady Holmes name mentioned a dozen times. I don't know what you're going to doing but if you need some help I've got my guns loaded."

"My friend, I really appreciate your help and we might need it. If the shooting breaks out here in town just keep an eye out for me, Bill Rose,

Pete Johnson and his men. Don't you fool around and get yourself shot. When this is all over I intend do a little business with you."

"You don't need to worry about me. I was in the little ruckus in that four year mess these blasted politicians got us into. You just watch out for yourself, you're the best paying customer I have." Carlen gave him a smile and extended his hand to the older man who shook with him.

The first stop was at Pete Johnson's ranch to get directions to the Grady Holmes ranch on the Utah border. Pete told him to come in and he would have his wrangler tend to his mounts. "Pete, I'm in a hurry to locate Bill Rose. I have a warrant to arrest Vernon Hull and I want to serve him in the Brown Mule Saloon."

"You just climb off of that pretty bay of Bud Wheelers and come on in and warm up. I can send one of my riders to fetch Bill before I could try and tell you how to get there. It's lunch time anyway and I hate to eat by myself."

Carlen handed the two horses to the wrangler and stomped the snow from his boots before entering the house. Pete was telling the yard man to send Willie Dean after Bill. Coffee was always on the kitchen stove. Carlen laid his hat and coat on a straight back chair and seated himself at the kitchen table.

"Well, Carlen, tell me of this warrant and whatever else is going to take place when you go after him."

Carlen told him in detail how he wanted to start with the arrest of Hull. Then do the search of the Brown Mule Saloon and Hull's home. When he was finished with those two he intended to search Farnsworth place and then the house in town and the ranch that Holmes owned. "Pete, I know that Bill and I are going to run into trouble. I don't know how many men that we are going up against. I'm going to need you and your riders to give us some help, especially at the Utah ranch."

"Carlen, you know that you and Bill can count on me. You just tell me where to be and when you want us there. I'll have all of my men ready except the six I left in town to keep an eye on the safe in Farris's store. There will be nine of us."

"Pete, if Holmes is in town when we go after Hull and Winfred Barnett, I'm almost sure that he will high tail it to the Utah ranch as soon as he figures out what's happening. You may need to post two riders there to see what his plans are. He might take some of what we are searching for and try to skip the country. Then he could come back to town with his crew of hard cases and try to free Hull. Should he do that, it's going to mean a lot of bullets will be flying around. One of the riders you station there could get back to town ahead of them and give us some warning. In case he tries to run, let one of your men trail him and mark his trail while the other man comes and give us the word that he is on the run."

"I think that's a good idea unless he already has that bunch of outlaws in town. We may be a few men shorthanded, but I can pull the three of the six from Farris's store."

"I kind of think that one or two of the people in town will come to our aid. The owner of the livery told me he had his guns loaded and was ready because he had a feeling there was going to be trouble in town before too much longer."

"Corky Rhodes sure ain't no youngster but he is as tough as a boot and is one heck of a good shot. He won't back up from anybody if he thinks he's in the right. I just hope we can get all of them in one clean sweep without some of us getting hurt or killed."

"Pete, my main concern is to get back all of the deeds and those missing ledger sheets. If we find all of them in the saloon we can only arrest Barnett. I hope that we find something in each search that would tie each one of them involved in the plot. If we don't then we have no proof to hold them on. "

Around three o'clock Bill and Willie arrived and Bill came to the house while Willie and the wrangler took care of the horses. "I guess that we got the word from Judge Hayes that we've been waiting for."

"Curtiss brought the warrants to the store and I had to get a hold of you before we start serving them. Pete and his riders are going to back us up if we need any help. The judge only got one name from the safecracker and the arrest warrant is for Vernon Hull. I want to arrest him in the Brown Mule Saloon so we can serve the warrant on Barnett and search his saloon and home. That way maybe we can keep the other two from being warned that we are after them. Pete can have men at the front door and at the back of the saloon to keep anyone from leaving until we search all three places. Then I think we should search the land agent's home and office and save Grady Holmes for last."

"Grady was just getting to the ranch alone when Willie came for me. About half of his twenty men were leaving for town as he arrived. They stopped and talked to him for a couple of minutes then rode on toward town."

"Pete, Bill and I will ride on to town and be waiting in the store watching the saloon. You wait about an hour then send your men where you want them stationed and then join us in the store. It should be good and dark by then."

"I'll be there with my riders; you two don't try to take that saloon by yourselves, just wait for us."

Chapter Eleven

The ride into San Juan was cold, but at least there was no wind or snow. Carlen left the bay at Pete's and rode his dun. Bill had put his saddle on a black horse that the wrangler told him was a good one. They rode in silence, each having thoughts of the coming drama that would surely cost a high price in blood and lives.

Darkness came early in the winter months and the town was lighted up on the plank walks when they arrived. "Carlen, I'm really hungry. I think that we have plenty of time and I hate to get in a fight with my tummy growling."

"Bill, I'm sure Betsy can find a little something that could fill us both up. What say that we give it a try?"

They tied up at the hitching rail in front of the café and found the place deserted. They seated themselves at Farris's favorite table. Betsy placed two cups of fresh coffee in front of them and Bill asked, "Where are all of your customers? I guess that you just got tired of getting no tips and you ran them off."

"No, not really, the tips were average for this time of the year and we've fed a lot of people today. About ten or twelve of them work for Grady Holmes. They were unusually quiet today. Most of the time they are a fairly rowdy bunch."

"Betsy, has Vernon Hull been in today?"

"Yes, he had supper about thirty minutes ago and two of Grady's men were talking with him about getting into a high stakes poker game at Barnett's saloon."

"How about Giles Farnsworth and Grady Holmes, have you seen them?"

"Holmes had lunch alone and left and I haven't seen him since. Farnsworth had an early supper and left just as Hull started in. They chatted about something on the porch and Farnsworth frowned and walked off."

They asked Betsy to fix them something of her own choosing. She did and it was very good. Carlen paid her and Bill placed a tip on the table. They bid her goodnight and left. Carlen told Bill that they should leave their mounts tied in front of the café where they would be less likely to catch a stray bullet. Bill agreed.

Farris still had a farmer and his wife doing a little shopping for a few things. The two marshals made good use of the heat from the front big coal burning heater and sat quietly until the farmer and his wife departed.

Farris walked over by them and said, "I watched Vernon Hull and two men who work for Grady Holmes walk into the saloon a little while ago. Curtiss was here with me and told me not to close up until he got back. I don't know what he had on his mind but he was looking very worried."

Corky Rhodes made the bell tinkle and grinned as he placed a ten gauge double barrel shotgun against the wall. "Well, I figured you two boys were fixing to open the ball when I saw you leave your horses tied up in front of the café. I didn't want to miss the first dance so I just loaded up my little old two row shotgun in case you fellers need some help."

Bill grinned at the hostler and replied, "Corky, we can use all of the help that we can get. You just make sure that cannon you are going to use is headed in the direction of the outlaws. I don't want the doctor picking buckshot out of my rear end."

"Bill, you ain't got to worry one bit about my shootin. You just herd them in my direction and I'll give them a real dose of lead poison."

Curtiss and Pete Johnson entered through the back door. Curtiss was carrying a Winchester rifle and had a walnut handle Colt stuck in his waist band. Pete told them that he had all of his men in position covering the saloon front and back and two of them watching the Utah ranch. "Carlen, do you think that Farnsworth will run if a lot of shooting breaks out?"

"I wouldn't doubt it one bit. Curtiss, would you and Corky keep an eye on him just in case he decides to get out of town in a hurry?"

Farris replied for Curtiss, "I'll go and help Curtiss. You need Corky here as you are outnumbered, and I still know how to shoot well enough to take care of myself."

The lawyer and store owner departed through the back door. Carlen told the others to give them a few minutes to get there. "Corky, why don't you stay here in the store where you can watch both sides of the saloon in case one of them decided to leave through one of the windows?"

"I can handle that little job easy enough."

"Pete, Bill and I don't want you to take a bullet so don't stand too close to us. I want Bill to keep a sharp eye on Winfred Barnett and you watch all of Grady's men. Should one of them look like he is going for his gun, don't hesitate to shoot him."

"I ain't got but six shells in this hog leg. I hope that there ain't more than six of them that want to try me."

Bill and Carlen grinned and Bill replied, "If there are six you have to shoot, be sure you don't miss a one of them."

"Don't you worry about this old man missing; they don't call me Dead Eye Pete for nothing."

Carlen told Pete to let them go in first and for him to come in a minute later. Carlen opened the front door and pushed the bat wings open and glanced around the room. He didn't recognize any town people in the half filled room. Bill walked a little way down the right wall and leaned against it where he had a clear view of the bar. Carlen spotted Vernon Hull at a card table playing poker with three men that he knew were Grady's gunmen. He started toward the table when Pete entered and stood at the front wall where he could watch the whole room.

Carlen stopped at the table and waited until the hand was finished. As the cards were shoved to the dealer he said in a loud enough voice so the four could plainly understand him, "You men leave your hands on the table. I'm a United States Marshal and I have an arrest warrant for Vernon Hull." It was so quiet you could have heard a fly walk across a window pane.

"Well, well, if it's not the apron wearing clerk in here to arrest me. What's the charge clerk, spitting on the floor?"

"You can argue the charge with Federal Judge Hayes in Durango, Hull. You can come peaceful or I'll drag you out, the choice is yours."

"Listen to this store clerk men, he thinks I'm going peaceful."

Pete's hog leg roared once then again and two men were a half a second apart entering eternity. Vernon Hull was the recipient of a forty four Colt barrel sleeping pill courtesy of an apron wearing clerk.

Bill's pistol put a bullet in the left hand of Winfred as he tried to bring up a sawed off double barrel shotgun from under the bar. Three men ran for the back door and Pete's riders let them get clear of the back steps before three rifle shots put them away for good. The one that jumped through the window was given a hard dose of Corky's medicine that was guaranteed to cure or kill. Too bad that it wouldn't cure. Oh well, what could a crook expect anyway.

Six of Grady's riders were dead and the other four decided that they wanted no part of the fight.

After the shooting ceased and the smoke filled room was clear Corky called out that he was coming in. "Well, boys, looks like y'all had a little trouble in here."

Carlen told him to go get the mayor, get the jail unlocked and light up the lanterns. "While he's doing that, Corky, bring us six pair of handcuffs. If you see the doctor on the street tell him we need him here."

"I'm on my way. I couldn't lock the door to Farris's store. I don't have a key."

Carlen reached in his pocket and pitched the hostler the key and gave him a wink, "Now you do."

The four men of Grady's were relieved of their weapons and given an all over search. Everything was removed from their possession except their tobacco, but no matches were allowed to be kept. Winfred Barnett went through the same search, complaining all the while of his bullet hole hand. Bill told him to him to shut up or he would shoot a hole in his other hand.

Hull was still in the land of nod when they searched him. They found a ring of keys that matched the ones they found on Winfred. Carlen put both rings in his pocket and Winfred asked him why he was keeping their keys.

"You and Vernon will find out soon enough. I'm sending these four other men to jail while Bill and I have a little sit to with you and Hull."

Then Corky arrived with the handcuffs and the four were cuffed, and then taken to the local jail by Pete and his riders. The good doctor patched up Winfred's hand and then he and Hull were cuffed.

Carlen pulled the envelope from his coat pocket and handed it to Barnett. "Winfred this is a search warrant that gives us the right to search your saloon and residence. I ask you to cooperate or we will take whatever measures are necessary to enter your safe and all doors and drawers that are locked."

"I haven't committed any crime that allows you to do this to me."

"Well, Winfred, you were just shot in the hand for trying to kill a U.S. Marshal. That alone guarantees you a date with the hang man. If you want to sulk up like a spoiled child we will be glad to take this place apart board by board."

"I don't have anything that you would want."

"The court will decide what is needed to place all of you four council members on the gallows. You are already going to be hung by the neck until you are dead, so why not cooperate with us?"

"I have nothing else to say to any of you."

"Corky, you keep an eye on these two while Bill and I tear this place apart."

The two marshals started with the safe in Winfred's office. It was an old safe with a lock in the handle. The ring of keys was all that they needed to open it. Placing the contents of the now empty safe on a table they sorted through the papers and put all of the money in a bank bag. Going through the papers, Carlen found the ledger sheet that had been removed from the county clerk's office that recorded the deed to Farris's store. Also was a bank balance sheet showing the money on deposit for the hardware and lumber yard.

Carlen walked to the front of the saloon and grabbed Winfred by the collar. He jerked him up from his chair and said, "Come with me, you've got some explaining to do." He showed him the ledger and the balance of the account of the lumber and hardware store on the night the bank was robbed. "Winfred Barnett, this is evidence that you not only robbed the bank but also you are guilty of stealing a recorded deed from the county clerk's office. I think I should let the owner of each one of these papers have a hanging party for you right here in this saloon. These people have placed their faith and trust in you and you have betrayed them. Some city councilman you are."

"I can't explain how they got there. I didn't have anything to do with any of this."

"Then why did you try to use that shotgun on me when I arrested Hull?"

Winfred couldn't answer. He just looked down at his feet.

"Come with me and join your cohorts in the county jail. You will be held there until Judge Hayes sets a trial date for the people in San Juan County to judge you."

Carlen told Bill and Corky to stay with Hull while he put Barnett in jail with the others. After he saw that Winfred was securely behind bars he told Pete of what they had found in the safe.

"Well, that was just about what you expected wasn't it?"

"I had hoped to find a lot more. I really thought that I would find your and Farris's ledger sheets there along with the others they had taken. I guess that they have divided up what they already have stolen. I'll bet you that Grady Holmes has the ledger sheet of the recording of your ranch. I'm going to leave Corky watching over Vernon Hull while Bill and I search the home of Giles Farnsworth. Just in case we hear shooting here at the jail we'll be here pronto."

"If Holmes tries to break these men out you don't worry about us. We'll just do to them what we've done to the others."

Back at the saloon Carlen told Corky that he and Bill were going to search the Farnsworth house and for him to keep an eye on Hull in case he was to wake up before they got back.

"If this sucker wakes up, Carlen, I'll put him right back to sleep."

"Just make sure that you don't kill him."

"I wouldn't do a thing like that. I want to see him swinging from the hangman's gallows with my own rope around his neck."

The home of Giles Farnsworth had the lamps burning in the parlor. Neither Farris nor Curtiss were anywhere outside the home. Carlen walked up on the porch and knocked on the door. He heard Farris call out, "Who's there?"

"Bill and Carlen, Farris, can we come in?"

"Open the door and come on in as there is just the three of us here having a little chat."

Carlen gently opened the door and could see Farnsworth bound hand and foot sitting in a rocking chair. Curtiss was on the couch and Farris was standing by the wood heater. Farnsworth asked, "What is going on, why did these two tie me up? I'm an employee of the government and I demand an explanation."

Carlen asked, "Curtiss, I assume that this man tried to leave town?"

"He tried, but he just didn't quite make it. Farris waited outside watching the front and I was at the back of the house. When the shooting started he got busy packing a few things and when he started saddling his horse I invited him to come back in the house with me. Farris heard us and told him we had come to visit. He told us where to go and put his foot in the stirrup. Farris, very politely, jabbed him in the back with his pistol and told him we were his guests and that he shouldn't treat us that way. He finally realized his mistake so we placed him in the rocking chair and made sure he let us visit for a while."

"Where are the things he was taking with him on his moonlight ride?"

"In the saddle bags on the kitchen table. I thought that he might offer to fix us some coffee but he doesn't seem to enjoy our presence."

Bill retrieved the saddle bags from the kitchen and handed them to Carlen.

One side of the saddle bags was filled with money. The other side contained several envelopes and a small metal box about a foot long and six inches wide and deep.

Farnsworth cried out, "Don't you dare open that box, it contains government papers that are none of your business. "

Carlen showed him the search warrant and told him that the judge that signed the warrant was an employee of the government also and ranked a lot higher up the ladder than he did.

Carlen opened the metal box and the first two papers he glanced at made him smile. He handed them to Curtiss. "Read the heading and then tells us what they are and to whom they belong."

Curtiss glanced at the two sheets and said, "One is the deed to the café owned by Wilbur Jones and his wife and daughter. The other one is a recording of the deed that was removed from the ledger in the county clerk's office."

"Well, well, Farnsworth. Just what business does a government employee have with these two valuable papers that are in your possession? Arrest him, Bill, and we'll haul his thieving carcass to the jail to join the rest of his friends. Bill untied him and told him that he was under arrest by U.S. Marshals' and that if he tried to escape he had better be faster than a bullet.

"Curtiss, if you and Farris don't mind, would you two take all of this evidence by the Brown Mule Saloon and take what we retrieved from there and place it all in the big safe in Farris's office? As soon as we get Farnsworth put away we will meet you in the saloon where Corky is guarding Hull."

Farnsworth really didn't like the idea of being locked up and Bill told him that they could hang him now and save the county a lot of expense. He told him jail would be fine.

The government land agent was surprised to see the jail lighted up and Pete Johnson wearing the badge of the county sheriff. After they had him locked up Pete told the two marshals that the mayor had stuck the badge on him and said, "Mister Johnson, since all of the council members cannot be present it is in my power to appoint you Sheriff of San Juan County and to swear your men all in as deputies."

Bill asked him, "Pete, who's going to take care of your ranch while you lollygag around town? I guess you know that the sheriff serves a six year term."

"I'll quit as soon as this mess is over with."

"You can't just quit when you have been appointed sheriff. You must serve out your complete term."

"Bill Rose, I might just make you sheriff and help Carlen wind this little job up in a hurry. All you want to do is set around here and be jealous because I'm the San Juan County Sheriff. Just haul your butt out of here or I'll go do your job for you, you hoorawing no good cowboy."

"I'm going papa, please don't whip me with that willow switch again."

Pete's men and Carlen got a good laugh out of the two humoring friends.

Carlen and Bill found Vernon Hull sitting in a chair with Corky across the table from him with his cannon of a shotgun pointed at his chest.

"This here no good sack of horse manure wanted me to turn him lose. He even offered me a thousand dollars if I would. I told him it was my money that he stole from his own bank that he wanted to pay me with. He's dumber than I thought he was."

Curtiss and Farris came in and Carlen told Hull to get on his feet. "Where are we going, Marshal?"

"I heard you call me an apron clerk an hour ago, what has made you repent?"

"I've just now realized that you are really a marshal, and I want to address you properly."

"Well, let's walk over to your house and see what we can find. By the way this is a search warrant in case you decide to argue about what we are going home with you for."

"I have no idea of why you want to search my home, Marshal. I have nothing of interest to you or anyone else."

"Well, if that's the case, I guess you don't know of the bank's deposits sheets with all of the amount of money along with the deeds and ledger from the county clerk's office have been found in two of your other council member's possession. I think you know quite well what we will be searching for. You are already going to hang so you might as well cooperate with us to save a lot of time and save having your house demolished in the search."

"I really have nothing to say of the matter, I have nothing of what you speak of."

"We are just going to make sure Hull, and if we find anything at all it will make you hang twice."

When they entered Hull's house Carlen told him to take a seat in a straight back chair. He asked Corky if he would mind keeping an eye on him while they searched the house. "Carlen, I would count it my pleasure. I hope he tries to make a run for the door. I haven't got to shoot but one of these crooks tonight and my trigger finger is mighty itchy."

The other four took a room apiece and started a thorough search of the house. After an hour of searching they had turned up nothing that would implicate Hull in the scheme of things. Carlen told them that he just had a feeling that evidence was here and they were just not looking in the right place. Curtiss told them that they had looked everywhere that money could be found. "I know that he offered Corky a thousand dollars to set him free so the money has got to be around here someplace."

Bill replied, "Well, I guess we had better start taking up the flooring boards and see if it's under the house."

Farris told them they might look in the attic first. "There is a cellar under the house. If one of you younger fellows will take the attic I'll take a lantern and search the cellar."

Carlen was a month younger than Curtiss so he and Bill took the attic through the lift up door in the kitchen. There was barely enough room for one man so Bill stood on the kitchen table with his head stuck through the door hole while Carlen searched the dusty attic. After seeing nothing except a few dirt dabbers' nest he told Bill that there was nothing there.

They left Corky watching Hull and went around back to the cellar. Farris and Curtiss had two bank money bags and were coming out of the cellar with a smile on their faces. Well Boys, Curtiss and I have found two big bags full of money but no papers at all."

Carlen replied, "I know that he has hidden his share of what they have stolen. Those deeds and ledger sheets are here some place. I'm going to see if there is anything or place where they could be hidden in plain sight."

They entered the house and Farris told Corky that they had recovered his money they had stolen from his livery stable account and a whole lot more.

"The quicker we get him hung the quicker I can get my money back. Curtiss, why don't you send a wire to the judge and ask him if I can be Hull's hangman? I want to see him dirty his britches when he hits the end of my rope around his neck." Hull didn't appreciate Corky's request to the judge.

Carlen studied each room of the six room home. Somewhere in one of these rooms were the papers he was seeking. To have Hull arrested and hung was not enough. He wanted to see the people of San Juan County get everything back that these men had stolen. He could not find any signs of the walls or floors being tampered with. He walked back into the parlor and glanced at a large painting hanging above the fireplace. He removed the painting from its hanger and saw where the cardboard backing had been loosened from the frame. He pried it open and pulled out a large flat packet manila envelope. He opened it and there were not only ledger sheets and deeds but an agreement of how the spoils of the money and property were to be divided.

"Well, well, I guess Santa Claus left these papers, deeds and the way you four councilmen were going to divide up all of the people's property and money.

"Men, we have found what we came for. Let's escort Councilman Hull to his new quarters in the county jail and proceed on to our next and last objective."

Chapter Twelve

Hull was quite surprised to see that they had Giles Farnsworth locked up. Pete wasn't to gentle with Hull when he shoved him into the last cell with no windows. "Hull, if it was still the good old days you wouldn't be here in this jail. You would already be swinging from a cottonwood limb. You should be thankful that we now have some real law and order in San Juan and the tax payers are going to pay for your food and lodging. I hope you enjoy your stay with us."

Back in the front office, Farris and Corky told the others that it was past bedtime for old folks and they bid them goodnight.

Pete asked, "Carlen, what's our next step?"

"Well fellows, Grady Holmes and his gun hands are all that's left. I think that you need to stay here with a couple of your men Pete. Bill and I will take four of your riders and meet the two that are watching Grady's ranch. That will make eight of us against him and the men he has left at the house. I don't know that we got all of his men that were here in town. One could have made it back to his ranch and warned him. That being the case, one of your riders should be here soon to let us know if he is leaving the country.

"Curtiss needs to stay in town as he is the only lawyer here. There may be some way that these crooks have notified a lawyer to come and try to bail them out. Curtiss can wire the judge in Durango and he can set bail or give Curtiss instructions on what action to take."

Pete replied, "Carlen, there ain't gonna be no two bit, shyster, jackleg lawyer gonna even try to get me to turn this mess of crooks loose. If one of them steps foot in this jail I'll lock that sucker up right along with his crooked friends."

"Pete, you have my permission to do it."

"Curtiss, now that we have most of the money, deeds and ledger sheets locked up in Farris's big safe, I need you to go through the deposit balances. If you would make a list of all who had money in the bank and the amount shown on their balance sheet, we would compare that total with the funds we have recovered. If Hull stole a lot of the money that was his personally we should have enough money to pay back all the depositors.

Pete named off four of his riders and told them to get saddled up and to go with Carlen and Bill. The men headed for the livery stable while Bill and Carlen retrieved their mounts from in front of the café.

About half way to the Utah ranch they met one of Pete's riders on his way to San Juan. The man pulled his horse to a stop and told them that a lone rider ran his mount almost to death coming from town. "We watched the house for an hour and Grady and his men roped out all fresh mounts and rode for the big canyon headed southeast. We counted ten men in all, including Grady Holmes. They had bed rolls and slickers along with grub sacks tied to their saddles. Grady had an extra pair of saddle bags which he tied across the front of his saddle. They all are armed with rifles and pistols. My partner is trailing them and marking the trail with short pieces of his rope tied to a bush along the trail. They have about a two hour start on us but I'm going to have to stop at Grady's ranch and see if I can get another horse, as this one is winded."

The men rode at a lope until they reached the ranch just at false dawn. A couple of men herded the loose horses into the corral and one was roped out to replace the winded one.

While the men were getting the fresh mount, Carlen and Bill searched the ranch house. They could tell that the house and bunkhouse were deserted in a hurry. Clothes were left hanging or scattered across the bunks. Grady's little safe was left with the door standing open.

"Well, Bill, I guess we know what he has in the saddlebags tied across the front of his saddle."

"Carlen, these men have a long start on us. We don't have any food or water for a long chase. I think that we should send the oldest man in Pete's crew back to San Juan and let him get two pack horses and load them down with supplies for a long drawn out chase. I know these canyons to the southwest of here pretty good. I hunted wild horses all over the south and west. I can tell you it is some of the most desolate and driest country a man can get into. There are a couple of trading post that serves mostly the Indians in the large reservations set aside for them. We will be lucky to find water for as many men that we have and the trading post doesn't carry much in the way of trail food. The packer should bring two half gallon canteens for each man.

"We can let the two of us go on ahead with what food and water we can get here, then let the others catch up with us. I figure they will try the old Indian trick of splitting up in pairs, then those two will separate and try to hide their tracks. They will travel like that for two or three days and all meet again at a good water hole to camp and rest. Most of Pete's men are pretty good trackers and I think they will stay on their trail. If they lose one set of tracks they will come back and pick up the tracks of the other man.

"After we've been on their trail a while I can almost bet I will know where they will all meet. Since water is so scarce there just aren't too many places to camp."

"Bill, this is your country and you just line us out and we'll get going."

Bill told the men of the plan and they all agreed. The oldest rider had roped a fresh mount out of Grady's corral and headed for town. The others started following the tracks of the ten outlaws.

The trail south was easy to follow through the reddish land. Bill kept to the trail with a lope to keep the horses from tiring to quick. After an hour he slowed down to a walk for a mile and then back to a lope.

They rode upon the place where their quarry stopped to have lunch and rest their mounts. Two men left the party and their tracks headed due west. "Well," Bill spoke up, "these two will be the first to reach where they plan to set up camp. They will more than likely think that all of us will stay with the eight men that are still headed south. One of us should trail these two and see if they try to circle and come back behind us. If they split up it will be a sure sign that they are headed for the camp site. I believe that our man trailing them will meet us before dark."

Carlen volunteered to go, telling them that if he should lose both sets of tracks he would come back and catch up with them. " If I can I will stay on the trail until they reach camp or stop on the trail for the night. I'll stay with them until they meet the others, and then back track them until I meet up with you fellows."

He mounted his big dun and started following the two sets of westerly bound tracks. He stayed with them until dark and then made a cold camp for the night. Bill wasn't kidding when he said the land would become desolate. After darkness swallowed up the landscape he searched the horizon for a camp fire. There was nothing that showed any signs of habitation. Carlen felt like he was the only person on earth. He shared half of his canteen with the dun then screwed the cap back on. He knew that the big horse was going to have to carry him many miles before this chase was finished.

As soon as it was light enough to see he was on the trail again. The only thing good was that this was winter time. In the summer the heat would take its toll on man and beast alike. At around ten o'clock he stopped where the two outlaws had spent the night. They left a couple of sardine tins on the ground and a small empty cracker box. He found only one set of tracks still heading west. He left the dun horse standing and started walking in a half circle from north to south on the west side of the dry camp. He then would widen the circle and walk back the other way. At about five hundred yards southwest he found the broken limb of brush that the rider used to wipe out his and the tracks of his horse. He had ridden the horse to where he had dismounted and tied the animal to a heavy brush limb and walked back to camp. He then walked backwards very carefully brushing all sign of man and horse. Carlen knew then that the man was going to head in a southwest direction to the camp site or join the others.

The tracks were easy to follow so he put the dun in a running walk that he could stay in all day with plenty of wind and strength to spare. He knew that he was closing in on the outlaw by seeing that his mount was starting to drag a hoof, kicking the ground forward a little more each time he pulled up his right forefoot.

Carlen kept his eyes constantly scanning ahead of him and off to the northwest. He wanted to spot either of the men before they spotted him.

Late that afternoon he saw the man he was following, walking and leading his sore footed mount. Carlen dismounted and waited for the sun to sink below the horizon then mounted and stayed in the trail until he spotted a small camp fire in the distance. He removed the saddle and rubbed the dun down with the saddle blanket and let him graze on whatever scant grass and leaves he could find. He knew that if the outlaw had seen him that the man would try to kill him and take his horse. It was a cold, long sleepless winter night. Just before daylight the outlaw stoked up his fire and Carlen watched as the man led his horse to the fire and lifted up the right front foot and examined it. The man then saddled the horse and started walking in the same direction that they had been traveling. Carlen waited until the man was lost from his sight, then leading his mount walked to the fire which the man never bothered to put out.

Carlen was in no hurry for he knew that he could catch up with the outlaw quickly. He kept scanning the country looking for any signs of life but there was none to be seen. He waited for a couple of hours and then mounted up and took the trail again. Around noon he had the man and horse in sight and suddenly they seemed to vanish. He rode on with caution thinking that he may have been seen. The man could have put his horse down and was hidden waiting to get a shot at whoever was trailing him.

He noticed that the land was changing. There were more rocks and washes and there were a few larger cedar and juniper trees growing ahead of him. Suddenly the trail dropped off into a deep wash and descended along the side of the wash to the bottom. The tracks of the man and horse were plain in the soft dirt as he looked up and down the wash but there was no one in sight. There was a bend about a mile to the west that turned the wash due south, so he figured that the man and horse were beyond the bend. There was no place for an ambush that he could see so he let his mount take the trail to the bottom. Before he reached the bend he dismounted and kept on the left side next to the wall. He looked around the corner and watched the man and horse stop at a stand of mesquite and willow trees. Carlen knew that there must be a spring or seep there for the man unsaddled the horse and made a small fire. Evidently this was going to be where the man would camp for the night.

Carlen knew that he would soon have to find water and feed for his horse and himself. He waited until sundown and looked again to see if the other rider might have joined the one at the spring. The man was saddling the lame horse and Carlen was hoping that he was leaving. It could be that there might be some Indians that wouldn't like for a white man to be trespassing on the land that the Washington politicians had so generously given them. In a few minutes the man and horse were out of sight in the winding wash that had become a canyon. Carlen mounted and rode to the cluster of trees. There was a small spring that emptied into a rock basin about two feet deep. Carlen and the dun drank side by side. The water was cold and had no taste of salt or alkali. Carlen washed out his canteen and filled it while the big dun chewed on the willow leaves.

He mounted and stayed on the man's trail until dark. The thought of a flash flood hit him like a bolt of lightning. Should there be a hard lasting rain; water could get deep in a hurry in the bottom of this canyon. Well, the sky is as clear as a bell and stars seem so bright and close you would think you could almost reach out and touch them.

Meanwhile Bill and the rest of the riders were waiting for the pack animals and the food and water to arrive. Grady Holmes had separated two more riders here where they waited. The rider that was marking the trail had waited here for help to arrive. He told Bill that Grady had slowed down and all of their horses were really tiring. Late the next afternoon the lone rider, leading his pack animals, rode into camp and the riders all enjoyed a good meal with coffee.

The next morning early, Bill sent two of Pete's riders on the trail of the two that had departed from Grady's main group. Bill figured that there were five men still with him. He had the feeling that this bunch was headed into Arizona Territory, maybe all the way to what people called the Grand Canyon. He wished that he could separate the hoof prints of Grady's horse from the others. There just wasn't any way to find out. All they could do was stay on the trail.

Bill had been scouting ahead when he spotted the head and shoulders of a man that was dropping down into a lower bench where he had once got caught in a bad dust storm. He watched the man's head and hat disappear then dismounted and walked leading his horse to where he could see the bench. Below the bench was a fairly deep canyon with a small stream winding through the rocky bottom. He had never been in the canyon but had followed the bench due west to where the canyon intercepted a much larger one with a small river running year around. He had a pretty good idea where Grady was going to hole up. The long narrow bench sloped down to the river's edge at the intersection of the two canyons. In the large canyon ponderosa pine and juniper grew in abundance. It was a little paradise in the middle of the wasteland. There was deer, elk and an abundance of trout in the river. A person could have a comfortable camp there for a long while. As he watched one of Pete's riders, who was tracking the two outlaws, began to wave off to his right, Bill mounted up and rode to the rider who had dismounted and was drinking from his canteen.

He told Bill that when the two men he and his partner were tracking split up, he almost knew that the hideout was going to be in this area. "I ain't never been in that river canyon but I've heard the old timers talk about it and where it was located. Bill, I think this may be a trail that's been too easy to follow. I've got a feeling that they are settin' up a trap for us. I ain't much of a tracker but I believe that a ten year old kid could hide his tracks better than this man did. I kinda figger that we may be caught between a rock and a hard place."

"Charlie, I truly believe that you're right. Anyone with common sense would know that seasoned men like we have in this posse would figure on a long trail. These men haven't even tried to fool us. I think that we had better do some Indian scouting before we go in there hell bent for leather. I wonder how Carlen is making out. He only had one canteen and a little jerky in his saddle bags."

"I wouldn't worry about him, Bill. That young feller has more savvy than a lot of the old men I know, includin' me."

"Well, let's get back to the rest of our men and get camp set up for the night. Maybe all of us together can come up with an idea on how to do this."

Carlen trailed the man ahead of him to another canyon intersection where a small stream of water trickled through the rocky bottom. The trail turned due west and he could see where this canyon that he had just entered ran into another one that turned due south. He watched from behind some huge boulders while the man crossed a fair size stream and unsaddled his horse and made camp. He guessed since it was the middle of the afternoon that this was where he would meet his companion. An hour before dark he heard a shod horse on the bench above him. He had the dun tied against the canyon wall, below the rider and out of his sight. Carlen watched with his field glasses when the rider crossed the stream and waved at the one in camp. He didn't know if this was his partner or not. About twilight there was another rider that came into the camp from upstream instead of the trail on the bench. He had a feeling that something was wrong about this setup. The man he trailed could have been followed by anyone. He thought the best thing to do was back track to where he entered the canyon and see if he could find Bill and the others.

He watered his horse and filled his canteen then rode back up the stream. He left the stream where the trail turned up to the beginning of the long bench. His dun raised his head and sniffed the cold night air. Carlen knew that someone or something was not far ahead. He heard a horse whistle in the distance. He dismounted and held the dun's nose to silence his reply. Carlen knew that the animal belonged to Bill and Pete's riders or to Grady Holmes and his hired gunmen. He walked, leading his mount in the sandy soil toward the sound of the horse's whistle.

There was a wash that ran toward the canyon that he had just left so he led the dun into it and tied him to a scrub mesquite. He quietly eased his way up the wash where it rounded a curve. He could see the embers of a camp fire about a hundred yards ahead. He could count the horses and knew that it was Bill and Pete's riders as Grady's gang didn't have this many mounts.

He gave a hello to the camp and was asked to identify himself. He recognized Bill's voice and told him that he would go back and get his horse and join them.

The others went back to their bed rolls while Bill and Carlen told one another of their thoughts. The packer had brought a sack of oats from San Juan and Carlen gave his dun a good feeding. He waited until breakfast to get the first real meal he had eaten in the last few days.

Carlen explained to the riders what he had seen and told them that he thought that Grady and his outlaws were planning an ambush. "The three men I saw in camp seemed to want us to find them. I may be wrong but it was just too easy to trail the man I followed."

Charlie said, "I told Bill the same thing late yesterday evening when we met at the beginning of the bench. I think that if we go riding down the bench or either of the two canyons they will just be waiting to bushwhack us."

Bill asked. "Carlen, what do you think we should do?"

"How far is it to where we can get a fresh supply of food?"

"There is a large trading post about ten or twelve miles south of Angle Peak." Bill drew a map in the sand and showed them the location of the trading post and where they were at now.

"We can head southwest and be there by mid-afternoon. We can get a good meal there and replenish our supplies. I think Grady and a couple of his men might be there. It's the only place around until you get across the border into Arizona. That would be a hard three day ride with no water, unless they met up with the three Carlen watched in the canyon."

Carlen told them he thought they should go to the trading post and buy enough supplies for a long trip. He told them that he would buy two more horses to pack on should they need to split up to follow the outlaws. That way they would have plenty of food and water with some grain for the horses. They all agreed that this would be the best plan.

They packed up the camp and headed for the trading post. Around three o'clock they had the trading post in sight. There were a few horses tied to the hitching rail in front of the store and several that were in the corral.

Carlen suggested that they check out the brands on the horses before entering the building. Bill and Charlie told them that they would ride ahead and tell them before they entered if any of Grady's bunch were there. The others dismounted and checked their weapons and killed time until Bill and Charlie finished. They watched as Bill waved for them to come on to the corral.

There were four horses in the corral that wore Grady's brand, but none at the tie rack. Carlen told them that he would bet that Grady made a horse swap here and was already gone. Carlen and Bill entered the building first and all that they could see were two cowboys and a few Indians. The rest of the men entered and they all found a place at the tables with benches.

The trader was an older white man wearing an apron and asked if they wanted to eat. "My wife is a good cook and we have a fresh pot of beef stew and plenty of fresh bread. I don't have any way to keep ice so you fellers will have to drink water or coffee."

The eight men all ordered the stew with coffee. While they were waiting to be served, one of the cowboys who Bill knew walked over to the table and shook hands with Bill. "You ain't out here in this neck of the woods wild horse huntin' are you, Bill?"

"No, Dewey, not this time, we're looking for Grady Holmes and about nine of his riders. I don't guess that you have seen him around here lately have you?"

"Bill, you're a day late. Him and three of his high dollar gun hands were in here yesterday and traded for four fresh mounts and headed southwest. I kinda figured that the law was on his tail the way they were watching their back trail. They didn't waste any more time here than they had to."

"Well, Dewey, for your information we are the law. Carlen is a U.S. Marshal and I'm a U.S. Deputy Marshal. These other fellows are deputies of San Juan County."

"By golly, Bill, I never dreamed that you would ever become a lawman. I guess you would make a good one with your common sense and the way you can handle a pistol. I hope you never have to get after me."

"The only person that we are interested in is Grady and his bunch. I don't guess he said anything about where they were headed, did he?"

"I had my head down on the poker table like I was drunk or asleep. The only thing I heard was that they needed enough water for them and their horses for four days. I did watch them leave heading southwest leading a burdened down pack mule."

They finished eating and Carlen bought two pack horses with pack saddles and panniers.

They filled all of their canteens and water sacks for the horses while the camp cook had all of the food packed. They purchased oats for the horses and let Bill and Carlen pick up the trail of the four fugitives. They made about twenty miles before dark and set up camp under a cloudy sky. The cook fixed up a quick supper while the others tended to the horses and gathered up fire wood.

They broke camp the next morning with little flurries of fine snow swirling around them. Bill and Carlen were back on the trail still headed toward the southwest.

"Carlen, I think that these four are headed to Chaco Canyon where there is water and graze for their animals. The other six are behind us waiting to see if we fell for their ambush trick. Since we haven't shown up there they will probably think that we have quit or figured out what they were trying to pull. They will wait another day and head for the canyon to meet up with these we're trailing. Maybe we should set up a little ambush for them and then Grady might surrender knowing that the odds are too strong for him to fight."

"Bill, how much longer will it take us to get to the canyon?"

"We should be there well before dark tomorrow if that is where this trail takes us."

"If you know the trail that the other six will come in on I think it would be a good idea. Should we be on the wrong trail and they get by us, that's going to make us have a long hard fight on our hands."

"There is a high rise on the northeast rim of the canyon and with field glasses we can see them for miles away. I don't think that this little snow is going to last long. If it gets too heavy and hides their tracks we're in trouble."

They pushed their mounts hard as long as the tracks could be seen. Supper was cooked and the horses tended to while the north wind blew a little harder. The horses turned their tails to the wind and the riders spread their ground tarps and rolled into their blankets.

At midnight the north wind had pushed the clouds to the southeast and the stars were shining bright. Before dawn the cook had breakfast ready while the rest had brushed down their mounts and saddled them. As soon as it was light enough to see the ground from the back of a horse they were on their way.

They kept pushing their horses hard, not stopping for a noon break. Two hours before dark they stopped with the rim of the canyon in sight. Bill and Carlen went on ahead on foot to see if there was any sign of the outlaws. With field glasses they could see the four horses and the mule hobbled in the floor of the canyon. There were rock houses built by Indians of long ago sheltered under the overhanging cliffs. The scene reminded Carlen of the ones at Mesa Verde. He could make out the abandoned field and garden areas with the irrigation ditches. Carlen wondered what happened to the industrious people who once lived here.

They rejoined Pete's riders and told them of what they had seen. Charlie asked, "What are we going to do now?"

Carlen replied, "I think we should wait until dark, then slip down there and steal their mounts and pack mule. That way they are stuck here on foot. We can leave two men here to keep an eye on them while the rest of us see if we can catch the others that will try to join them. I would like to try to take them alive, but the choice is theirs. They may think that we have already taken care of Grady and the other three and surrender without a fight."

Bill said, "After it gets dark I think we can see their cook fire. They shouldn't be camped to far from where the horses are hobbled. Once we have them located it will be easy to keep them in sight. I don't think they will keep a guard posted tonight. We have gained a day on them and they won't be expecting us until sometime tomorrow."

Finding a wash where their fire could not be seen they made camp and waited until dark. After a hot supper they left two men in camp and made their way down to the canyon floor. Each man carried a rope to bring out the captured animals. By midnight they were back in camp with the four horses and the mule. Charlie said, "I wish it would all be as easy as this little job was."

An hour before dawn Carlen, Bill and four of the deputies rode out of camp to watch for the six men they thought would be coming to meet their cohorts.

When they reached the base of the hill that Bill told them they would watch from, he dismounted. "Men, Carlen, and I will watch from the top of this rise. You take our horses and hide yourselves in that draw to our right. Loosen your cinches and don't build a fire. We will take us a bite to eat. If we see anything we'll be down this side where they can't see us."

The two marshals climbed to the top and made a brush blind to hide them from any view of the oncoming outlaws. Carlen told Bill to catch a little sleep if he wanted to and he would take the first watch. Two hours later they traded places and Bill took the watch. About two o'clock Carlen gave Bill a whistle and he was instantly awake. Carlen pointed in a northeast direction and handed Bill the field glasses.

Bill said, "Carlen, I count six riders without any pack animals."

"That's the same count I had. I guess that these are the six we've been waiting for."

"Well, they will come between us and Pete's riders. Let's get down and get the others spotted in a good position for an ambush in case they don't want to surrender."

They left their mounts tied in the wash out of sight and Bill took two men with him and placed them on the west side of the trail. Carlen and the other two took the east side and found places for protection from the expected bullets.

Their wait was over an hour before they watched the six mounted men come around the side of the hill. When the men were even with them Carlen stood up and yelled out, "You men are surrounded by the law so get your hands above your heads. If anyone of you reach for a weapon you will be shot."

They were in single file on the narrow trail and the lead rider slipped to the west side of his horse Indian style and spurred the animal into a quick start. That was a big mistake. Bill put a bullet in him and he dropped from the running mount. The last man had turned his horse and was running back the way they came from when Charlie's bullet knocked him from the saddle. The other four decided they had better not try anything. While Pete's riders kept them covered Bill and Carlen took their weapons and searched them, removing any knives and hideout pistols. They then hand-cuffed them and tied their hands to their saddle horns. They then loaded the two dead ones on their horses belly down and took them to their camp.

Bill unlocked two of the outlaws and made them bury one of their dead comrades. When they finished he cuffed them again and made the other two bury the other one.

They then packed up and moved back to their base camp for a hot supper. After eating, Carlen took two sets of leg irons and secured two men together. He told Bill that they would keep a two man watch on these four at all times. "We still have a little daylight left so I'm going to see if Grady and the other three are out looking for their stolen horses."

Carlen eased up to the edge of the canyon and with the aid of his field glasses searched the canyon. The only place he could see where water might be was at the base of a high cliff where there were cottonwood and willow trees growing. He felt like Grady would not be concerned if his men didn't arrive tonight. One or two more days would make him understand that something had happened to them. He watched until the light faded away and returned to camp.

When it was light enough to see he was back scanning the canyon for any sign of Grady and his men. At a time like this a man has a lot of time to think as he watched. His thoughts turned to Peggy Fletcher. She was the only woman in his life that he would ever love. He fully intended to keep the promise he made to her. When he saw this bunch of crooks either dead or behind bars he was going to buy a ranch and never be a lawman again. Carlen was the only child of his parents and when they died they left him well off. The funds from a ranch that he sold in Texas would purchase just about anything that he wanted and stock it with enough cattle to make he and Peggy a good living. He knew that he wanted to settle in San Juan County. The people here were the salt of the earth. He knew that he had to see Bud Wheeler and buy the bay horse, if Bud would sell him, or return him and pay for the rental. Back in Mancos Bud wasn't the least bit worried about the horse. His greatest concern was the safety of Carlen Ashton.

When the sun light covered the canyon floor Carlen watched a man come from behind the cottonwood and willow trees and look across the canyon. He walked out to where he could see most of the canyon then turned and walked at a fast pace to the trees. In a few minutes three more joined him and were looking in all directions across the canyon. Well, they finally had discovered that their mounts and pack mule had disappeared. This brought a smile to Carlen and gave him a feeling that they probably wished they had put a guard to watch their method of transportation. The four split up and started searching where the animals could have gone. One man found where they lost their hobbles and waved the others over. Carlen knew that they would see the boot prints left by the horse thieves and wondered what they would do next.

He eased out of their sight and walked back to camp and summoned Bill to come with him. He told him of what he had seen and they went back to watch and see if the outlaws would try to track their trail. Carlen told Bill where they came from and Bill told him that was the only good water in the canyon. "There is a small rock house in behind the trees. I guess that's where they have their camp. I think we have enough food to wait them out, but water is our big problem. That spring down there is the only one I know of that's got good water."

"Well, Bill, we can slip down there tonight and keep them inside the house and that way we will have the water for ourselves. I'm hoping that Grady will send the three men to try to find their mounts and we can capture or kill them. Then Grady will be the only one left to worry about."

As they watched, two men started following the boot and horse tracks. "Bill, if you want to keep an eye on the two in the canyon I'll get a couple of Pete's men and see if we can capture these trackers."

"Carlen, send two men over here with me and tell them to bring my rifle along with theirs. If we can get to the rock house before they do, we will have this chase over with."

In ten minutes the two marshals were on their way in opposite directions. Carlen told Charlie to pick one man and take Bill's rifle and plenty of shells for all three and give Bill a hand.

He took two of Pete's riders with him and went down the wash where they had brought out the stolen horses. Just before they reached the canyon rim he told the two men to get up the bank of the wash and find some cover and watch for the two men following the tracks. Carlen told them if they chose to fight instead of surrender they would have to kill them.

Bill and the two riders with him hurried along the canyon rim out of sight from the two outlaws on the floor of the canyon. When they reached a wash running into the canyon they left the rim and entered the bottom of the canyon. From here they could be seen by their adversaries. They slowed to a walk hopefully making the outlaws think that they were three of Grady's men. They reached the trees and took cover to where they could have the outlaws boxed into keep them from reaching the rock house.

Carlen watched as the two men tracking the stolen horses came into view up the wash. When they were even with him and Pete's riders Carlen said, "You men raise your hands. You are under arrest by U.S. Marshals. Don't try for your weapons or you will be killed. Lay belly down with your arms and legs spread out." The two looked at the three rifles pointed at them and followed instructions. Carlen told his deputies to climb down and disarm them while he kept them covered. After a thorough search they marched the two back to camp and chained them to the other four.

Bill and the two riders watched as Grady Holmes and his companion came strolling toward the rock house. When they came through the trees on to the clearing Bill told them to raise their hands above their heads. "You two men are under arrest by U.S. Marshals." Seeing that there was no chance to fight their way out they were disarmed and searched. Bill told the two deputies to guard them while he searched the house. "If either one of these two look like they want to make a break just kill them."

Bill found the saddle bags and the contents were just what he expected. He left everything else where it was and returned to their base camp. Grady and the other man were locked in with the others. He asked, "Where are my other two men?"

Bill replied, "Where you are going to be after you finish your time on the gallows."

Grady didn't ask any more questions.

The outlaws were under guard at all times with a change of guards every two hours. A false dawn breakfast was finished and the journey back to San Juan began. The first night was spent on the trail and the second at the trading post.

Dewey came in after dark and visited with Bill. "Well, it looks like you caught up with all of them but two."

"Dewey, the other two didn't seem to want to face up to what was in store for them so we just laid them to rest. They won't break any more laws on this good earth."

"Bill, all of the ranchers in this part of the country will be mighty thankful that you fellows have finally put a stop to Grady and his bunch of rustlers. I wish that I could have been with you."

"Dewey, if you need a job, you should see Harvey Crowell. He is a few men short and could use your help."

"Are you going to be a marshal the rest of your life?"

"No, I sure like being a lawman, but when these men are tried a long with the others Carlen and I will be finished. This is the only job that I have ever had that I felt like I was accomplishing something worthwhile."

After they all had a breakfast, cooked by the trader's wife, they started again on the trail home. At the noon hour of the fourth day the residents of San Juan watched the cavalcade enter town.

Sheriff Pete Johnson had more men in the jail than it was built for. Carlen wired Judge Hayes in Durango and told him of the arrest and of the overcrowding of the town's jail. Judge Hayes replied that he was on his way to San Juan to prepare for their trial.

With the evidence that was compiled against them Curtiss told Carlen and Bill that none of the men could escape the gallows.

"Fellows, I really feel sorry for the lawyers who have to try to defend this bunch. I will be the prosecuting attorney and I fully intend to see that they all hang. I don't think that the judge will have a bit of trouble picking out a good honest twelve man jury that will convict all of them."

Chapter Thirteen

The entire county of San Juan was ready to hang the whole bunch without a trial. When the local newspaper printed the story of all that had been planned by the four council members there was disbelief at first. By the time the truth got around to all of the property owners they were mad.

Judge Hayes arrived and so did the hard case defense attorney from Durango. The first thing he told the judge was that there was no way to find an impartial jury in the state of Colorado. The judge totally agreed with him so he called on the next door neighbor, The Territory of New Mexico, to furnish the court citizens whose property was not involved in this case. That put a quick stop to the defense attorney's complaint. He didn't like it but there was nothing else he could say.

This was Curtiss's first big trial and he made sure that he had proof of every charge against the councilmen and Grady's hired guns. The only proof he didn't have was who killed the last sheriff of San Juan. Well, he would try to find that out when he quizzed the rustlers on the witness stand.

Since there was no bailiff in San Juan, Judge Hayes called the court to order himself. After asking if the defense and prosecuting attorneys were ready, he called in the first of the hired gunman. Of course the man pleaded not guilty to all of the counts against him. By the time Curtiss got through with his questions the man hardly knew what he said or where he was. Judge Hayes was proud of Curtiss Fletcher being a member of the bar. The last question Curtiss asked the man was, "Why did you kill our last sheriff when you stole Pete Johnson's cattle?"

The reply, "I didn't kill him, Rio Barnes did."

The defense attorney almost fell out of his chair then jumped up and objected.

"Objection overruled. Please sit down and try to control yourself sir," replied the judge.

Curtiss turned the witness over to the defense, who knew better than to ask him a question.

Summations' were made and the case went to the twelve man jury. In a little less than an hour they returned with a guilty verdict.

Judge Hayes, with the accused standing, looked him straight in the eyes and said, "You have been found guilty of cattle rustling and aiding in the murder of a local sheriff. Two other men in the posse that tried to stop you were severely wounded. By your own testimony you have admitted to being a part of this rustling and killing of innocent people. I hereby sentence you to be hung by the neck until death claims your mortal body and may the Good Lord have mercy on your soul."

The seven gunmen of Grady's that were captured in the canyon and the four that were captured in the Brown Mule Saloon received the same sentence as they were tried one by one. Judge Hayes closed the court for the day and told them he would reconvene the trial at nine o'clock in the morning.

Grady Holmes entered the court-room handcuffed with Pete Johnson on one side of him and one of his deputies on the other. The court-room was packed with the people of San Juan County. There wasn't enough room to seat one third of them. Judge Hayes asked them to let those standing in the aisles and against the walls to trade places with those seated when he called for a recess.

Grady had a defiant look on his face while he listened to the charges against him. Bill Rose was called to the witness stand and sworn in. After stating his name and occupation he was asked by Curtiss to describe the chase and capture of Grady and his men. Bill told of the chase and final capture of Grady and his hired gunmen. He went into detail of the two saddle bags he found in the rock house and of their contents.

The defense attorney tried every way to trap Bill into a mistake or an all out lie. Bill never changed a word and never batted and eye as the lawyer hounded him until Judge Hayes told him to finish with the witness now.

The defense lawyer called Grady to the stand to testify in his own behalf. That was a very bad mistake. Grady swore that he knew nothing of the charges against him and that they were a pack of lies. His lawyer painted a picture of Grady to be a God fearing rancher that was arrested by mistake and all charges should be dropped and the court apologize for his arrest.

The accused was handed over to Curtiss for him to question." Mister Holmes, you claim that you know nothing of the plot your friends on this city council asked you to join them in; to seize this town and county?"

"Yes, I had no knowledge of this you're accusing me of."

"Then please tell the court how your were the guardian of all of the money, deeds and ledger sheets that were stolen from the county clerk's office,"

"I have no idea of how they got into our camp house in Chaco Canyon."

"Your Honor, I would like to excuse this man and reserve the right to recall him if necessary."

"Permission granted; the witness is excused."

Curtiss looked at the deputy that helped Pete escort Grady in and called him to the witness stand. After he was sworn in, Curtiss asked, "When Grady Holmes and his men left after being warned of the gunfight and arrest in San Juan, where were you stationed at?"

"My partner and I were watching Grady's ranch house over close to the Utah border."

"Would you please explain to the court in your own words what took place there?"

"Before Pete was sworn in as San Juan's sheriff Carlen told him to send two men to watch the ranch house and see if Grady made a run for it when he started arresting the three other council men. I picked out Jimmy to go with me because we had worked together for several years. While we watched, a rider came in from the direction of town and in a few minutes Grady and his gunnies where catching and saddling horses. They packed food in flour sacks and tied them and canteens on their saddles. Grady came out of the house carrying a pair of saddle bags in his left hand which he tied in front of his saddle. I sent Jimmy back to town to tell Carlen that they were skipping the country and I followed them, marking the trail for the others to follow."

"I hand the witness to the defense, Your Honor."

The hard nose lawyer tried in vain to get the witness to change his story. Finally the witness asked him, "Mister Lawyer, I have told you the exact same thing every time you ask me. Are you hard of hearing or don't you understand what I'm saying?"

This brought a roar of laughter from the crowd and Judge Hayes smiled as he rapped his gavel on the desk and asked for quiet. The defense attorney just resumed his seat with a hard frown on his face. Judge Hayes excused the witness and asked the lawyers for a summation.

The case was handed to the jury and the judge called an hour and a half recess for lunch.

Judge Hayes, Carlen and Bill had lunch in the Judge's chambers and when finished discussed Grady's defense. Carlen said, "Judge, we have in Vernon Hull's papers that we found in his house, the written agreement of the four on how they agreed to split up the town and county. Grady's signature is on the agreement along with the other three. I don't know why Curtiss didn't enter it in evidence. It lists the property that matches the deeds and ledger pages we found in the saddle bags Bill found at their campsite in the canyon."

The judge replied, "I don't understand either but Curtiss has his reasons. I'm sure that the jury will find Grady guilty. We already have the testimony of his rustlers admitting that he ordered them to rustle Pete Johnson's cattle when the sheriff was killed. That alone will get him the death sentence."

Bill spoke up, "Your Honor, we need to either hang these men quickly or have about half of them moved to Durango. The jail here is so overcrowded now that it's getting hard on Pete and his men to keep them from trying to kill one another. The place is getting to stink and we need to do something as soon as possible."

"What would you and Carlen suggest?"

"Either hang Grady's six gunnies here tomorrow or ship them to the big jail in Durango. I don't know of anything else we can do."

"Well, I'll postpone the trial for three days until the town can build a gallows and get the six hung. I'll make the announcement as soon as I convene the court. You two marshals see to it that the gallows is erected quickly and properly."

The two marshals left as soon as they finished lunch and went to the lumber yard. They explained the order given them by Judge Hayes and the owner told them that he would gladly donate the time and labor and have it built and ready to hang the six by the day after tomorrow. By the time they told Pete of the Judge's plan to hang the six there was a wagon load of lumber and four carpenters in the vacant lot next to the jail. The owner was a man of his word.

Pete's prisoners didn't pay much attention to the building going on until one of them looked out the cell window and said, "Oh my Lord, they are building a six man gallows." The rest of them were crowding to have a look see as the Indian would say. A sudden silence fell over the cells as the outlaws realized that their time on earth was growing short, very short. Giles Farnsworth started shaking like an aspen leaf in the wind. Tears started running down his cheeks. He sat on his cot and buried his face in his hands and sobbed like a child. Breaking the law is a very hard lesson to learn. Well so much for getting rich in a hurry.

When he stopped shaking and crying he told Vernon Hull that the big idea he had to steal the town and county wasn't working out to well. Hull replied, "You other three were just as gullible as I was. If it wasn't for that Texas lawman we would have been on easy street. I wish that the two men that Grady sent to kill him had gotten the job done." Winfred Barnett told him, "Vernon, you just wish in one hand and spit in the other and see which one fills up the fastest. I ain't worried too much about the dying. I'm really worried if that preacher is right about the fiery furnace he always is preaching about." His little speech put quite a few of them to thinking.

At ten thirty the next morning Pete and two of his deputies came into the cell block and told the eleven of Grady's gunmen to stick their hands between the cell bars. One by one they were handcuffed and with two shotgun guards covering them they walked in single file to the unpainted gallows. Since San Juan had no hangman the job belonged to Pete. One by one they climbed the thirteen steps to the platform. With the guards watching, Pete placed a black hood on each of the outlaws and then slipped the hangman's noose around their necks. Not a word was uttered when Pete pulled the lever, six men dropped instantly. After hanging for twenty minutes the doctor pronounced them dead and they were placed in the undertaker's wagon. The local preacher, the town doctor and the newspaper editor were the only three in attendance. Another twenty minutes later the town undertaker and his assistant removed the ropes and loaded the last five in the bed of a wagon to make them ready for burial. Well, the jail wouldn't be nearly as crowded.

Judge Hayes let another day pass before calling the court back in session. When he rapped the gavel on the desk there was a hushed silence over the filled court-room. The judge called the jury from the ante room and asked if they had reached a verdict on Grady Holmes. "Yes we have Your Honor, we the jury find Mister Holmes guilty of all charges."

Judge Hayes asked the defendant to stand to hear the sentence. "Grady Holmes, you have been found guilty of the charges against you. By the power invested in me I hereby sentence you to be hanged by the neck until dead. Date of your hanging will be set after the last accused of your partners in this trial are tried. Sheriff, please return the defendant to his cell."

Pete and his deputy escorted Grady back to his clean cell without a word spoken between them. The next man to be tried was Giles Farnsworth. When Pete told him to place his hands between the bars he refused. The deputy unlocked the cell door and Pete walked in and said, "Farnsworth, you can come like a man should or I'll have you carried out. You ain't half of a man. You're just a great big overgrown baby. Stick out your hands or I'll crack you over the head with this billy club and pack you out over my shoulders to the court-room wearing nothing but a diaper."

Winfred Barnett told Farnsworth that Pete would do exactly what he said. "You have got to go one way or another. Why don't you act like a man for a change and take your medicine like the rest of us?"

Farnsworth stuck out his shaking hands and Pete snapped the cuffs on him. On the short walk to the court-room he asked Pete what sentence was given Grady. Pete replied, "The high dollar rustler and killer got exactly what he deserved." Farnsworth didn't have to ask what that was.

The Jury didn't take long to find a guilty verdict after the attorneys finished their summations. Farnsworth took the death sentence like a man should. The judge called for a noon recess and said that court would start the next session at two o'clock.

A while before it was time for court to convene, Pete called for Winfred Barnett to get ready for the cuffs. The saloon owner stuck his hands through the bars without hesitation.

Pete and one deputy walked him into the court-room and they sat alone in the empty building. Winfred spoke to Pete, "Pete, I want to thank you for the good talks we had before I got mixed up in this mess. I always knew you were one of the finest men I ever met. The way Vernon Hull explained this to me was way over my head. I wish I had come to you before I joined up with these other three. I know that I'm going to hang and I deserve it. I don't want you to think I blame you or anyone else. I was dumb enough to get involved with them and I intend to take my medicine like a man."

The court-room filled up and the judge entered and opened the session. Before the judge could even ask the attorneys if they were ready Winfred stood up and asked, "Your Honor, may I speak before we begin?"

"Mister Barnett, if your speech has anything to do with these proceedings you may, if not I ask you to take your seat."

"Your Honor, what I'm going to say has everything to do with this trial. I am as guilty as a man can be and I don't want no jackleg lawyer trying to sway the jury with his highfalutin' speeches. I plead guilty to the charges against me. I want to thank Bill Rose for shootin' me in the left hand to keep me from trying to kill Carlen Ashton. I have committed no murders and haven't given anyone my permission to do so. What I did to the good people of San Juan I ask their forgiveness and I'm ready to hear you sentence me to hang right along with the other three councilmen I was dumb enough to join up with. Thank you."

Winfred took his seat and there was absolute silence in the room. Judge Hayes ordered the jury to the ante room and called for a thirty minute recess. He asked Pete and Bill to join him in the ante room and for Carlen to stay with the deputy and the prisoner.

In the jury room he asked each one the same question, "Gentlemen, was Winfred Barnett sincere in his request?" Every one of the men had known the saloon keeper for a long time and each of them told the judge that he meant what he said.

"Pete, do you think that he was making this speech just to gain the sympathy of the jury and the crowd in the court-room?"

"No, Your Honor, he was just telling it like it is. I've known him a long time and had a lot of conversations with him over the years and I know he meant what he said."

"Marshal Rose, how do you feel about this man?"

"Sir, I'm like Pete, I've known him for a long time. He has staked me a couple of times when I was broke without me even asking him. I never figured that he would pull that shotgun on Carlen. I'm thankful that I was good enough shot to hit his hand. I just couldn't kill him."

"Gentlemen, we have already hung eleven men here and one in Durango. I have no idea how many have been killed in the gun battles here or elsewhere concerning this case. We have three more in the jail that we are going to hang when this trial is finished. I think that we should give this man a thirty year sentence without parole. I know that he will most likely die before he completes his time but I can't bring myself to sentence him to hang." All fourteen men agreed with the judge.

When the judge returned and the jury seated, Judge Hayes told the defendant to rise. "Mister Barnett, the jury and I have reached a decision due to your apology to the people of San Juan County that we will not sentence you to death. You are to be placed in the state prison in Canon City to serve thirty years without parole. I hope that this will be a lesson to you when you re-enter society. Court is adjourned for today."

When Pete and Carlen walked Winfred back to jail he thanked Pete for his help. Pete told him not to say a word to the other three. "Vernon Hull is the last one we have to get before the judge and there is no reason for you to let them know anything. I'm sure that the judge will send you to Canon City as soon as he can. I think he will hang the others before you leave."

"Pete, I sure thought I was going to hang for sure. I just wanted to tell all of the old boys who were my friends for years how sorry I was to try a fool stunt like this. I hope that they and the Good Lord will forgive me for being so stupid."

"Winfred, we all make mistakes, if I had a dollar for each one I have made I'd be a rich man. You just made a great big mistake instead of the small ones like I have made. When you get to Canon City keep your nose clean and show respect for the guards and the warden. What do you want me to do with your saloon while you're gone?"

"Pete, you talk like I'm just leaving town for a month or two. I don't have any kin to give it to so I'll just deed it to you."

"What in the Sam hill is an old cuss like me going to do with a saloon? I don't drink anything except a beer or two a year."

"Well, Pete, you are the best, most honest man I know here and I want you to have it. You can sell it or close it down. If you sell it give the money to the local church and that poor skinny preacher. Tell Curtiss to come by the jail, I really need to talk to him."

The next morning the last of the thieving minds was waiting on the judge to get his trial under way. Curtiss had visited Winfred at the jail and was primed to see Vernon Hull get the justice that was due him.

The judge entered and called the court to order and seated the jury. Curtiss put everything that they had found in the search of his house on the desk top of Judge Hayes. The most damming piece of evidence was the agreement that Hull had drawn up to how the properties and money was to be divided. It took him twenty minutes to read it to the jury and the people in the court-room. Curtiss never called anyone to the stand. He didn't have to. The defense lawyer made a real fool of himself trying to rebuff all of the charges that Curtiss rendered to the court. When he finally finished the judge asked for a summation and Curtiss rose and said, "Your Honor, I can see no reason to carry this matter any farther, the facts are undeniable. This document was written by Mister Hull, the other three men have testified to this. Your Honor, the prosecution rest."

The defense lawyer tried to earn his money but couldn't. After a ten minute plea for lenience he closed.

Judge Hayes sent the jury out to decide the fate of Vernon Hull and an hour recess was called.

At the end of recess Vernon Hull received his sentence of death by hanging. Court was adjourned.

Two days later Winfred Barnett stood at his cell window and watched the three men pay the penalty of their crimes. The gallows had served its purpose.

Chapter Fourteen

Judge Hayes told Pete to assign two of his deputies to escort Winfred to Durango and then take the train to Canon City. He handed the necessary papers to Pete and gave him government vouchers to pay for their expenses.

He asked Curtiss, and his sister Peggy, to meet him in his chambers at eleven o'clock. When they arrived Carlen and Bill Rose were there. The judge had asked them to meet him in order to get all of their cost receipts so he could reimburse them. Carlen told him he didn't have a receipt from Bud Wheeler because he had not taken the bay rent horse, saddle and rifle back. He wanted to buy the bay if Bud would sell him. The judge told Carlen that he would settle up with Bud when he got there to catch the train from Mancos to Durango.

The judge spoke, "Curtiss, I'm proud of the way you handled the job of prosecutor for the court. I have this voucher here for your time and I added a little for expenses. The people of the State of Colorado thank you."

"Miss Peggy Fletcher, this voucher is payable to you for the sum of twelve hundred dollars. One thousand is for the reward of the outlaw you shot to save the life of Carlen. The two hundred is the money the man had on him for payment to carry out Vernon Hull's orders. This is not blood money. The man was a wanted killer of women folks. You have probably saved not only your life but the lives of other ladies as well."

"Curtiss, I have spoken to Mayor Todd Simpson and as of today you will sit on the board of council for the town and county of San Juan. The mayor will set your salary and you will be responsible for taking and caring for the minutes of each meeting."

"My two marshals, Carlen and Bill, there is no way that myself or the people of San Juan County can thank you both enough for what you have accomplished to save them from total disaster. Since you both have tendered your badges to me I can have you both reinstated and you can work out of the Denver office. I am giving these badges to Curtiss to hold in case either or both of you are needed in the future. Being a member of the bar, I have given Curtiss the power of attorney to swear you in on temporary duty."

Carlen replied, "Your Honor, I thank you for the offer in Denver, but I'm going to find a ranch in this area and settle down here for the rest of my life. I will be ready for any temporary duty if I'm needed.

"Bill Rose, how about you?"

"Sir, I was proud to serve as a marshal but this area is my home. I couldn't be happy anywhere else. I, like Carlen will be glad to help for short term duty."

"As a favor to me, I want both of you two ex-marshals to attend the first meeting of the new town council."

"I believe that we have concluded our business. I'm going to treat all of you and Betsy Jones to a steak dinner at the hotel dining room."

The next morning Carlen had breakfast with Judge Hayes before he departed on the stage to Mancos. A week later Carlen received a letter from Bud Wheeler, enclosed was a bill of sale for the bay horse and a receipt for a saddle and a 45/70 Winchester rifle. Bud's note told him it was one way that the judge said he could thank him for being his marshal for a little while.

The new town council was made up of Mayor Todd Simpson, Pete Johnson, Farris Baker and Wilbur Jones with Curtiss Fletcher as secretary and legal advisor. Bill and Carlen were the only others in the meeting room.

Mayor Simpson brought the meeting to order and told the group that acting Sheriff Pete Johnson had resigned in order to see over his ranch. The main purpose of the meeting was to replace the departing sheriff. The mayor said, "Carlen, I made you the offer once to become our sheriff. Would you reconsider and take the same offer and be our sheriff?"

"No, Mayor, I have made other commitments. I can recommend a man whom I have worked with in law enforcement that is as qualified as I am. I hope that he will accept your offer."

Pete Johnson stood up and walked over to Bill Rose and said, "Bill, its time you settled down and made something out of yourself. Carlen says that you're the man for the job and if he says you will make us a good sheriff, you can do it."

Bill Rose was sworn in as the Sheriff of San Juan County.

Carlen knocked on the door of the Fletcher residence and was greeted by Peggy. She asked him in and when he closed the door she folded in his arms. He held her tightly and then she kissed him and said, "Carlen, I'm so thankful that this bad time is all behind us and you are mine from now on."

"Peggy, I'm going to ride out to Pete's ranch and bring back my bay horse. Saturday is day after tomorrow and if the weather is not to cold or snowing I thought you might want to take a little ride."

"Aren't you going back to work for Farris?"

"I told you when I finished my job with Judge Hayes that I was yours. I meant what I said. I want you to ride with me and we will look for us a place to buy, get married and settle down. I want to own a ranch and be your cowboy, if you agree to my desires. You won't need to teach school and I won't be an apron wearing clerk. Our lives will be our own to make what we want to out of them."

"Carlen, I think that will be wonderful. I have never thought about being a rancher's wife until you mentioned it a while back. I have no idea of what ranch life will be like. I hope you don't expect me to work cattle and be a housekeeping mother too."

"No, I just want you to be content and happy."

"How large of a place do you intend to buy?"

"As large as I can with the funds that I have. That's why I want you to go with me and help me pick out a place that we both like. It will need to have good grass and plenty of water."

"I'll dress warm and have us a sack lunch fixed and be ready early Saturday morning."

Carlen saddled up his dun at Corky's livery stable and headed for Pete's ranch. It really felt good to be back in the saddle again. The crisp morning air was fresh and the scent of pine was strong as he rode through the forest up to the never ending bench. Carlen had no idea of how much land Pete owned. Carlen thought it would really be nice to find a place like Pete's.

He dismounted at the tie rack at the back of the house and the wrangler shook hands with him telling Carlen that Pete was in the big house complaining about his arthritis. Carlen took the steps up the back porch and Pete's Chinese cook opened the back door. He gave Carlen a slight bow and told him Pete was in the parlor setting by the big fireplace.

When Carlen entered the large room Pete started to rise from the overstuffed chair and Carlen told him to keep his seat. Pete sank back down and told Carlen to drag up a chair and make himself comfortable.

"Well, Carlen, what's going on in the big city of San Juan? I figure that you're out here to tell me that Bill Rose has already resigned his post as sheriff."

"No, Pete, Bill is going to make the county a great sheriff. I think that his wandering days are over. I came to visit you for two reasons. First, I came to pick up my bay horse and second I want you to guide me on a ranch to purchase. One with year around water and good grass and where I can build a nice home. The water is really the most important thing."

"How big of a place are you looking for?"

"Large enough to run enough cattle to make a good living on for Peggy and me. I guess around ten thousand acres to start with. I need to make sure that I have enough funds left to buy the stock with and to live on until I raise enough beef to drive to market."

""Carlen, I'm getting to old to run as many cattle as I do and I have more land than I need. How about we take a ride one day and I'll show you a dandy place that I have never grazed and it has three strong creeks running through it with several springs. There is plenty of good timber and an easy way to drive your cattle through the mountains to Durango to ship them. I wish that you and Peggy would come and live with me. You could run this place and be my foreman but I know how much a man wants a place of his own."

"If the weather is not to bad on Saturday Peggy and I will ride out here and you can show us what you would care to sell. I just hope that I can afford the price you ask. I don't believe in debt, it seems like once a man starts borrowing he can't seem to stop."

The Chinese cook placed two slices of dried apple pie and two cups of coffee on the small table. The two men finished the treats and Carlen told Pete they would see him Saturday if the weather was good. He and the wrangler placed Carlen's halter and lead rope on the bay and Carlen gave him a wave and left for San Juan.

Carlen tied the two mounts up in front of Farris's store and told him that it was lunch time and for him to go eat while he watched the store.

Farris didn't argue as he was really hungry. Farris had told Carlen that the apartment was his to live in as long as he wanted to. He really hated not to go back to work for his former boss but he just wasn't cut out to be a store clerk.

After Farris returned, Carlen rode to the livery stable and told Corky to take care of his two horses because he wanted to catch Bill before he went to eat lunch. Bill was telling the new hired deputy that he was headed to the café to grab a bite of lunch. "Bill, I was just coming to get you and buy your lunch. I want to talk to you about buying a little of Pete's ranch."

The two men sat at the back table next to the kitchen door. Betsy gave them both a smile as she placed their water glasses on the table. "Well, Bill, how is our new sheriff today?"

I'm fine, Betsy, I was wondering if my credit was good here but Carlen told me it was his day to buy."

"Bill, you know that your meals are paid for by the town. Since you and Carlen saved our café for us this dinner is already paid for."

Carlen replied, "Betsy, you can't just go giving your meals away. You know that you must make a profit to stay in business."

"Well, if it wasn't for you two we wouldn't have a business, so I'm treating you two to the best steak dinner you will ever eat."

The steak was the best as was the pie and coffee. After they finished Carlen told of the conversation with Pete on the piece of property he wanted him and Peggy to look at.

"Carlen, I know exactly where he is going to take you. He got a patent on that land by going through the government when they put the Ute Indians on the reservation. He promised the old Indian Chief that he would never graze the land himself but would give it to his son if he ever had one. The old Indian died several years ago and Pete still holds to his promise. I believe Pete thinks of you as the son he never had."

"Well, Bill, I sure think a lot of Pete and Farris too. They are as good and honest of any men I ever had any dealings with. I want to be fair with Pete and pay him what the land is worth. I wouldn't want anyone to think I'm trying to take advantage of him."

"Carlen, Pete's got more land and money than he knows what to do with. You or no one else could take advantage of him even if you wanted to. He has more cattle than all of the other ranchers combined in this area. I've seen him help a lot of people get a start in this county. He has a heart of gold for anyone who is honest and trying to better themselves."

"Bill, how do you like being sheriff? I knew that you had what it took to be a lawman so Pete and I laid it on the line to the new city council. All of them knew you well and agreed that you were the man they wanted. I personally think that the job will grow on you as you see the good you're doing for the town and the county. If I can ever be of any help to you all you need do is ask."

"Carlen, this is the first job that I ever had that I really wanted. I want to thank you and Pete for the recommendation you gave me."

Saturday morning before good daylight Carlen and Peggy were having breakfast with Betsy and Curtiss. Peggy told Carlen that she had bought her a pair of long johns, a wool lined coat and a wool scarf from Farris. The jeans and wool shirt would help ward off the morning chill. As soon as the meal was finished they picked up Carlen's two horses from Corky. Carlen adjusted the stirrups to fit Peggy and placed the sack lunches in their saddle bags. They left town at a fast walk to let the mounts warm up.

Pete was expecting them and had a fresh pot of coffee ready. The hot coffee took away the early morning chill as the sun started melting the light frost. "Well, Miss Fletcher, are you ready for a day's ride?"

"I'm ready, Mister Johnson, I've always been an early riser and I love the outdoors. The bay horse that Carlen got from Bud Wheeler is a dream to ride. He has the easiest gait that I could ask for. I've packed us a few things for lunch and Carlen has brought us a coffee pot and three tin cups. He has a couple of canteens of water so we are fixed and ready to ride."

"My horse is saddled and is at the hitching rail at the back of the house; let's be on our way."

Pete took them due west for about thirty minutes and when they came to a small valley he turned due north and stopped at a fence at a narrow neck of the valley. "Carlen, would you open the gate and close it when we get through?"

Carlen dismounted and opened the gate and closed it and could see the valley open up to a wide vast expanse with a strong flowing creek meandering through the valley. Cured grass was knee high and the slopes of the mountains on each side of the valley were covered with pine, spruce and aspen. Pockets of oak brush with service berry bushes were abundant at the base where the mountains reached the valley floor. The valley seemed to never end as the horizon met the earth below. Pete showed them a deep saddle on the eastern side of the valley and told them that there was an easy trail that circled the back of his range and intersected the trail to Durango that came out of San Juan. "Carlen, it's about five miles from where we are to town if you use this trail and if you turn due south where we entered the valley it's about three miles. You two would be less than an hour from my place. I have never grazed any stock on this valley. I made a promise to an old Indian Chief that I would save it for my son if I ever had one. I just never found a woman that would have an ornery old cuss like me. The Indian has been dead for several years and I sure would like to have you and Miss Peggy for neighbors. I don't need the land and would like to see it put to good use by someone who would be a good steward to it."

"It sure is a beautiful valley, Pete. If Peggy likes it and we can afford to pay the price you want I'm ready to make a deal."

"Well, let's ride on down here a way. You get us a fire going and get the coffee boiling and we'll talk about it."

Peggy spread a blanket from her saddle bags and Carlen built a small fire. When the wood burned down to a bed of coals he set the small pot on them and filled it with water. In a few minutes he placed in a measure of ground coffee and let it come to a boil for a minute, then set it off the fire and poured in a half a cup of water to settle the grounds. Peggy had the sack lunches spread out and the three enjoyed the meal in the fresh air and sunshine.

"Pete, how much land is in this valley? It seems like it never ends, with these side canyons there must be several thousand acres in here,"

"Well, Carlen, I had the government surveyor stake out all of the corners and years ago I stacked a rock cairn around the metal stakes. The entrance where we came in has an easement to the road going to San Juan. The trail leading out to the road to Durango is deeded with the land in the valley. There is plenty of ranch land in here for you two young people to have all of the cattle that you want to have. I don't rightly remember exactly how many sections are here but it's plenty for what you want to use it for. I have never seen the creeks or springs dry up in the droughts we've had since I've been here."

"Pete, just how much would it take for me to buy this hidden valley?"

"Carlen, I figure that if I could double my money for what I paid for it I would be a happy man. I've held it for many years and have never used it. I paid the Indians five thousand dollars for it and if you are willing to pay me ten thousand I would be well satisfied."

"Pete, don't you think that's just a mite too cheap. I'm sure there are others around here that would pay you more than you're asking me."

"Yes, Carlin, I could probably get a little more, but I'm awful particular who I sell it to. I want to know that my neighbor is an honest and trustworthy man. I don't figure I could find two more people like you and Miss Peggy if I looked the world over."

Peggy gave Pete a big hug and kissed his whiskered cheek and told him how much she and Carlen appreciated him.

"Well, let's mount up and go to San Juan so your brother Curtiss can draw up the papers. I'm thankful that I finally am going to have a family living here that feels like they are my own."

Chapter Fifteen

Monday morning Carlin and Pete sat in Curtiss's office signing the papers on the sale and purchase of the ranch land. After the papers were signed Carlen shook Pete's hand and thanked him for selling the property to him and his bride to be. "Just when is this wedding going to take place? Me and my riders want to plan a wedding party for you two and invite the town. I want to give you two a little gift."

"Pete, I guess I had better get on the ball and ask her when she wants to tie the knot. I have wanted to wait until I had purchased us a place, but that's all taken care of now. I'll see if I can find a good crew of carpenters to build us a house like she wants. We can rent a place here in town until the house is finished."

"There ain't no sense in doing a thing like that when you two can use that house that I built for a foreman that I never had. The place is clean and furnished and you two can ride out and check on the cattle you put on there and watch your home being built."

"Well, I guess I'd better talk to Peggy first before we make any plans to do anything just yet. She might want to wait until school is out before we are married. I don't want her mad at me until we are married and not then if I can help it."

Curtiss spoke up, "Carlen, I don't think she will be upset too much about what plans you make. She may not talk to you for a month of Sundays but she'll get over it. You will find that there is going to be a big change in your life being married to my sister."

Pete said, "Curtiss, don't be too hard on Carlen, Betsy might make a few changes in your lifestyle too."

Carlen and Peggy had supper at the Jones Family Café and he asked her when she would like to be married. "Carlen, I'm ready right now. The sooner the better as I don't know if Curtiss will allow me married and live in his house. I wouldn't want to anyway. I don't think Farris would like for us to have the store apartment either."

He told her about Pete and his riders wanting them to have the wedding at his ranch as he wanted to throw them a big party and invite the whole town.

"He also told me that he had a house built for a foreman that he never had and we can use it until I can get us a home built on our place. The only thing that makes it a drawback is that you will have to quit your teaching job."

"I was planning on quitting anyway. I want to spend my life with you and help you anyway that I can. I'm sure that there is some qualified teacher they can get to replace me."

Farris came in and they asked him to join them. "Well, how are you two young people this evening?"

Peggy answered, "We are fine, Mister Baker, and how is the best merchant in San Juan County?"

"I guess I'm as well as can be expected. I sure miss my clerk. I had the best sales day I have had since I opened up the store. It's beginning to get the best of me. I'm going to have to find a good reliable person to take Carlen's place or sell my store. I hate to sell it. I think I wouldn't trust anyone else to run my business because of the friends I have made since I've been a resident here."

"I was just telling Carlen that as soon as we are married I'm leaving my position as the school teacher here. I've been thinking about a friend of mine back home that I've been writing to. She graduated with me and married right after I came to teach here. She married a nice fellow who has a job as a traveling salesman for a dry goods manufacturing company. She told me that he wanted to find a steady job with no traveling. She could take my place at the school and if he meets your requirements he may be your answer to a good clerk. I'll send her a wire if you are interested."

"Peggy, that would solve both our problems. I just hope that the young man doesn't turn out wanting to be a cowboy."

"I'll send her a wire this evening and see if they might be interested."

"Farris, I feel guilty about living in the store apartment since I'm not working for you anymore. I need to pay you a rental fee since I'm staying there."

"Hogwash, Carlen, the service you have done for me and the rest of San Juan County has a thousand times paid for the apartment. I would consider it a favor when you two are married just to stay there."

Peggy told Farris of the purchase of the land and Pete offered them the use of the foreman's house until they could have their own built. "We'll be close to where we are planning to build and Carlen wants to purchase some cattle as quickly as he can."

After the meal was over the couple went to the telegraph station and sent a wire to Gladys and Kelly Cleveland in Memphis, Tennessee explaining the opportunity of permanent work in San Juan. The next afternoon when Peggy started home from the schoolhouse she stopped to see if there was a reply to her wire. There was, telling her they would leave within a week and travel by train to Mancos, Colorado. Peggy wired her back telling them to see Bud and Mother Wheeler at the general store in Mancos to catch the stage to San Juan. She then stopped at the store and told Farris that the couple would arrive in about two weeks. Farris was delighted to know that he had a prospect of hiring a trustworthy clerk.

Peggy and Carlen agreed to wait until the couple arrived to have their wedding. "I would love for Gladys to attend. I have asked Betsy to be my maid of honor and you need to pick someone to be your best man."

"Peggy, I don't know much about all of these arrangements. You are going to have the pleasure of doing all of the planning."

"Well, since my father has passed away, I am going to have Curtiss give me away. Why don't you ask Bill Rose to be your best man?"

"I can ask him and if he agrees you will have to tell both of us cowboys what we are supposed to do."

"Don't worry about a thing. I can handle everything including you and Bill on what you're to do."

Carlen started looking for a good line of beef cattle to start stocking the ranch. He visited with Harvey Crowell to see if he might have a few head to sell. Harvey told him he could sell him a few hundred head but they would have to wait until the time of the spring roundup. Harvey's wife, Sara, asked him when the wedding was going to happen. He told her that he didn't know for sure because Peggy was waiting for a couple from her home town that was coming.

"I guess as soon as they arrive Peggy will set the date and start sending out invitations. I'm sure that Pete Johnson will put an announcement in the local paper. He told me that he wanted us to tie the knot at his ranch. He said that he was going to invite the whole county."

Sara replied, "Knowing old Pete he'll really throw a shindig for you two. You might expect it to last a couple of days. Farris will lock up his store and the Jones family will do the same with their café."

"Folks, I didn't know that it took a party like this just to get married."

"Carlen, we out here in San Juan County don't get to visit much and something like what you two are fixing to do is call for a big get together. You and your bride might as well expect to get ready for it."

Two weeks and a couple of days passed when the afternoon stage pulled to a stop in front of the San Juan hotel. A dust covered man stepped out and extended his hand to help his dust covered wife to the ground. Curtiss and Peggy were on the hotel porch and came to meet them as they climbed up the porch steps. Hugs and handshakes were exchanged as the four renewed their friendship. Kelly and Curtiss gathered up their luggage and carried it up to the second floor suite they had reserved for their friends from back home.

Peggy said, "I know that you are tired and ready for a good bath and rest. Curtiss and I will come by around six this evening and we will have supper together."

Gladys replied, "That will be great, Peggy, as it has been a hard three day trip from Mancos. We should have rented a buggy from Mister Wheeler. That stage coach is not the best way to travel."

Peggy and Curtiss walked over to tell Farris that the couple had arrived and for him to have supper with them at the Jones café at six o'clock. "How about, Carlen, have you seen him today?"

"No, Farris, I haven't, I'm sure that he was out at the ranch property locating the best place for our home to be built on. He told me that we needed a place close to a strong spring of good water so it could be piped into the house. I think that Pete would go with him, knowing where the springs are located. I hope he gets back in time to have supper with us."

Carlen left his big dun at the livery stable and Corky told him that he would take care of his mount. "Carlen, you better get on down to see Farris. I watched Peggy and her brother meet two people that got off the stage this afternoon. Then they went to see Farris. I bet it's the couple that you folks have been expecting."

"I bet it is to Corky, thanks for letting me know. I'd better go get cleaned up. I figure that they will all be eating pretty soon."

As soon as he walked into the store Farris told him of the couple's arrival and for him to be ready for supper in about thirty minutes.

Carlen took a bath and shaved then dressed in clean range clothes. He couldn't see the need to dress up. He was a cowboy and the couple should understand that they were in the west which was the way most range people dressed. He waited until Farris was ready to lock up and walked with him to the café. "Carlen, I hope that I can put half as much trust in this young man as I have in you."

"Farris, you didn't know me from Adam when I walked into your store that early morning. Just give this young man a chance like you did for me. He may make you twice as good a clerk as I did."

"Carlen, you're one in a million. I could see it in your eyes when you first spoke to me. It seems like I have been blessed for I can nine times out of ten tell what kind of a person they are as soon as I meet them."

"Well, just remember that these two young people have just made a long journey to get here. You might want to wait a few days before you pass judgment on either of them."

"You're right, Carlen. I'll give the man every chance in the world. I just hope that he can make the grade that I expect of a good clerk."

The four were seated at a table for six when Carlen and Farris arrived. Introductions were made and hands were shaken. When the men were seated Betsy placed their iced water glasses on the table and handed each a menu. Carlen glanced at Kelly Cleveland and could tell that he spent most of his time in doors. He was a likeable fellow with wit and a taste for good humor. Gladys was friendly and asked a lot of questions about the country, town and school. After the meal was finished and they sipped another cup of coffee Farris asked, "Kelly, have you had any experience working in a general store?"

"Yes, Sir, I have. My father owned one back home and I worked for him until he sold it a year before Gladys and I married. I didn't care for the new owner so I found employment with a company in New York that made all kinds of wearing apparel. The job required a lot of travel away from home. I have been trying to find a place where Gladys and I were happy and I could find a decent job that let me be home."

Farris replied, "Well, Kelly, I'm in need of a clerk that I can easily train on how I operate my business. I'm getting to old to do it alone anymore. Carlen was a Godsend to me but he just wants to be a rancher and a cowboy. If you're interested I would like for you to give it a try and let's see if you are happy with me and I with you."

"Mister Baker, as soon as Gladys and I can find a place of residence I will be happy to start."

"Carlen has been staying in a nice apartment in the store and when he and Peggy are married you two can look it over and if it satisfies you both you're welcome to use it as long as you are happy with your job and can fill the position I expect of you."

"That's very nice of you, Mister Baker. Gladys and I can stay in the hotel until the wedding takes place. I just pray that the members of the town council will accept Gladys as a replacement for Peggy when she resigns her teaching job."

"If your wife has the qualifications that Peggy has there will be no problem. You can start work at the store as soon as you're ready, Kelly."

"Mister Baker, I'll be there the first thing in the morning."

"Just meet here at the café at seven-thirty and we'll have breakfast together."

Farris paid the bill of fare to Betsy and Carlen left a five dollar tip on the table for her.

Carlen walked Peggy home and he told her to get the date set for the wedding. "Just as soon as the weather warms up I'm going to have the carpenter crew start building our new home. You need to draw up a plan on how you want the rooms arranged and how many you think we need. I have talked to Bill and he agreed to be my best man."

"Well, the newspaper comes out day after tomorrow so why don't we make it Friday of next week. That will give everyone a week's notice if that's what Pete wants to do."

"I'll ride out there in the morning and tell him our plans. I'm pretty sure that it will be fine with him. I'll come back and tell you what he wants to do. I guess that the local preacher will perform the ceremony, if that's alright with you."

"Yes, I really think that the parson is a good man and his wife is really friendly."

Early the next morning Carlen put his saddle on the bay horse and rode out in the chilly morning to talk to Pete. Pete was expecting him and had the coffee hot and the cook was cooking up a ham and egg breakfast. Carlen explained Peggy's plans and Pete told him that he had an announcement prepared for him to take to the local editor and tell him to put it on the front page of the paper in big letters. He gave the note to Carlen and handed him a sealed envelope and told him to give it to Farris. "Carlen, I want you and Peggy to have a real western wedding. I have a few things planned that I hope surprise you two. You and Peggy are as close as I will ever have to a family of my own and I want to enjoy myself watching you two young folks tie the knot."

Carlen thanked Pete and told him that he would bring him a copy of the newspaper as soon as it was printed.

Carlen stopped at the general store and said hello to Farris and Kelly. He gave Farris the sealed envelope and told them he was going to the newspaper office to have them place the announcement and invitation in tomorrow's edition.

Chapter Sixteen

The next week was one of the most hectic in Carlen's life. Pete's announcement and invitation took up the entire front page of the paper. Everyone he met on the streets or any store he went in there was someone always congratulating him. Peggy had coached him and Bill until they had everything they were to do down pat. The ceremony was to start at one o'clock. The only place of business that was open after nine that Friday morning was the saloon that Pete had leased out to an old cowboy too old to punch cattle. He was shooing the last customer out so he could close.

The road to Pete's ranch was a steady stream of horses, buggies, wagons and buckboards. Pete's big storage barn with a wooden floor had been cleaned and scrubbed. His piano had been brought from the parlor and placed on the stage. The stage was raised a foot above the regular floor. Benches were placed in order to seat all that was possible. The men folks would stand against the wall. The preacher's wife sat at the keyboard and played music that most of the cowboys thought was meant for a funeral. At one sharp she started the wedding march and the services were under way. The preacher preformed the ceremony by memory. Bill, Curtiss and Carlen's parts went off without a hitch. When the doing was done, as Pete would say, Carlen kissed his partner for life and the end was over and the beginning started.

In the open faced shed, tables were spread with all kinds of good eats furnished by those who attended. Pete's riders had slow cooked two fat grain fed calves over the open pits. As soon as the feast ended the benches were placed long ways against the wall of the storage barn. Several of the men from San Juan County were gifted with musical talent. The preacher's wife could play anything from a waltz to a hoedown. It was time for an old fashion barn dance. Not a soul complained. Cowboys stood in line to just get a few seconds with one of the ladies before one of his friends cut in.

At five o'clock Pete called a halt to the music and told everyone it was time to bring in the gifts for the newlyweds. Almost everything to cook or eat with was given. Hand stitched quilts with wool woven Indian blankets, bed sheets, pillows and pillow cases.

Farris had a wagon backed up to the large doors and four of Pete's riders carried in a shiny black Monarch kitchen cook stove. Carlen was kind of embarrassed but Peggy had tears of thanks and happiness on her face. No matter how large or small the gift was she hugged and thanked each giver with the same affection. Carlen shook hands and thanked each one but when he came to Farris, the older man hugged him with tears in his eyes and said, "Carlen, it's me that should be thanking you." Carlen returned his hug and told him that being his friend was more than payment enough.

The days were getting a little longer as spring was coming soon. The late evenings were cold enough to have a fire. After the crowd had departed Peggy and Carlen sat in the parlor of the big house with Pete. The young couple thanked him for the most perfect wedding that anyone could have and how much everyone enjoyed it. "Carlen, I didn't want to let anyone know what my gift for you two was. I want to give you something that will give you both a start in life. I've had my riders round up a thousand head of three year old mother cows with calves and twenty five young bulls. We drove them into your pastures yesterday."

"Pete, I just don't know what to say. You have done more than enough for us as it is."

"Son, I'm an old man and I'm just about worn out. The last thing I need or want is two thousand more head of cattle next year. You two have each other and a son and or daughter to look forward to. All I have is just more cattle. The girl I wanted to marry before I came out here didn't want to leave her parents behind. So I just told her to grow up and be an old maid. I never even thought about getting married until I was too old. By that time I was used to being alone so here I am now all by myself and regretting it."

"Pete, you're a long way from being alone. You have more friends than you can count. You are the patriarch of San Juan County. You are the most respected and gracious man I have ever known. My parents have passed away as has Peggy's so we look to you as part of our family, as small as it is. You and Farris have been like two fathers to me. You two gentlemen are the foundation that holds San Juan County together."

"Carlen, when I look back at my life I would have given all I have, if had a son like you."

"Well, Pete, I'm just a man like the rest of us. I had a good upbringing and I try to treat others like I was treated as I grew up. You remind me so much of my own father."

The young newlyweds told Pete good night and as they started to leave he said, "I expect you two to have breakfast with me around seven thirty and I've told my riders not to harass you two tonight like we used to do ."

"Thanks, Pete, we'll see you at breakfast."

The next morning, while finishing a second cup of coffee, Carlen told Pete that he needed to buy a buggy and a buckboard. "I know that sooner or later we are going to need both of them. I guess that Corky's would be the best place to start looking. I'll buy a team that can be used for either of the vehicles, that means a harness set too."

"Carlen, you will use the buckboard a lot more than the buggy. I would advise you to buy a two seated buggy with a good top and side curtains on the buggy. That will keep you two drier and warmer in rain and cold. You can never tell if I might want to ride to town with you and Peggy once in a while."

"Pete, anytime you want to go we'll be ready to take you wherever you please. I'll buy four warm lap robes in case it gets really cold. Farris has some that will repel water. Would you like to ride into town with us this morning and see what we can find?"

"If you don't mind puttin' up with a grumpy old man, I'd love to."

Peggy replied, "Pete, you have never had a grumpy day in your life."

Corky could fix them up with all but the harness and lap robes. Corky was a horse trader and Pete loved to find flaws in what he had for sale, especially horses. The two old friends started in, one would try to dicker on the price and the other would shake his head. Peggy got to laughing after an hour and finally told them to come on and Carlen would buy all of them a hot lunch. Corky said, "I think that's the best news I've heard since Pete got here."

"Corky, old friend, you know that I ain't even got started yet. Just you wait until I get a chance to run them two old nags down the road a ways to see if they ain't wind broke."

Peggy told both of them to hold off on their dealings until after lunch. Carlen was just smiling.

As they entered the café Farris was just fixing to seat himself at his private table. Carlen asked him to join the crowd if he could put up with the rancher and the horse trader. Farris said he would love to.

Betsy served them and believe it or not Corky and Pete held their peace. Carlen felt a deep kind of kinship with these three men. In all of his short years in public life he had never had friends like these men were.

Carlen, with Pete's help finally settled on buying a pair of matched gray eight year old geldings. Carlen wound up buying a new buggy and buckboard. The used ones that Corky had for sale were just plain worn out. Carlin retrieved the harness set and four lap robes from Farris's general store and harnessed the team up to the buckboard. Peggy was still doing a little shopping and visiting with Farris and Kelly. He picked her up and had their two saddle horses tied on the back, headed for the ranch. Pete got through blabbering with Corky and caught up with them before they got out of town.

Pete told Carlen to put the buckboard in an empty stall in the wagon shed. He unhitched the team and placed the double harness in a gunny sack and told Pete and Peggy that he was going back to town and get the buggy. The wrangler had unsaddled the bay horse that Peggy rode to town. Carlen tied the sack of harness on the big dun and leading the two grays left to bring the new buggy back.

By the time he returned and stored the buggy away, then took care of his horses, Peggy had supper ready at their house and Pete was eating with them.

Chapter Seventeen

July the fourth was coming around soon and the town council was planning a big to do for all of the folks in San Juan County and their neighbors south of the river. It was to be a two day affair with fireworks display on the night of the fourth. Several of the local ranchers had agreed to furnish and have their cooks to barbeque enough fat steers to feed everyone. The ladies of the community were to bring the rest of the food and desserts. Coffee and iced tea would be furnished by Jones's café. A dance would be held each night after the festivities were finished.

This was to be a gala time for all ages to celebrate the birthday of the greatest nation on earth.

A week ahead of time preparations were under way. Twenty steers were in the corral at Corkey's livery stable. Ten chuck wagons were parked in nice neat rows under the giant cottonwood trees along the river banks. Pits were dug, oak and mesquite wood were cut and stacked by each pit. Wooden picnic tables were placed end to end on the fresh cut grass in the shade. Serving tables where all of the dishes of food were to be placed were ready. The freighter from Durango was at the lumber yard unloading the cartons of fireworks that had been ordered.

The evening of July second the steers were butchered and cleaned to be ready to start being slow cooked the next morning. The morning of the third, canvas covered wagons started to arrive and parked at their designated spots. Families would use these for their home away from home as the hotel and boarding house could not begin to accommodate the amount of people who was expected to attend. Bill Rose walked the area and shook hands with the men and welcomed them to help the County of San Juan celebrate.

Pete Johnson had weeks ago reserved two rooms at the hotel for himself and the Ashton's. His whole crew was to come and bring five wagons with canvas covers spread over the wooden bows in case of a rain, giving them a dry place to sleep.

Old friends shook hands and slapped one another on the back while the women folks hugged one another and enjoyed getting to see some that they hadn't seen in a long while.

'The morning of the fourth the local musicians played military marches and just before the noon meal was to be served they played the National Anthem. Hats and hands were placed over hearts and tears flowed from many eyes. It was a time to remember all of those who had given their lives for them to have and enjoy the freedom they were celebrating.

The afternoon wore on and after supper was finished the fireworks was ready and waiting to light up the night sky with noise, color and sights that would remain in children's memories until next year.

The dance lasted until midnight and the next morning sore toes and blistered feet were soaking in Epsom salts. Cowboys who were not used to walking more than a few feet a day were the ones who suffered the most. They all agreed that it was well worth the pain. The day finished and the night dance began again. You would never have thought that there was a sore foot in the crowd. After daylight and a breakfast was served the wagons, buggies and buckboards started on the road home.

Pete rode in the buggy with Carlen and Peggy while his crew followed in the five wagons. The Chinese cook was the only one at the ranch for the last three days.

Carlen had built a sturdy corral for the twenty five bulls that were given to him by Pete. The corral was built at the opening of a small canyon where the animals could graze and have access to a small creek. He left Peggy at the foreman's house that Pete was letting them use until they had their home completed. On the ride to check on his bulls he found the gate to his land was open and cattle and horse tracks filled the narrow road through the gate. He tied his dun horse to the fence so he wouldn't disturb the tracks and walked to his corral. The gate was open and the bulls were gone along with his cows. He started back to Pete's ranch as thunder boomed in the west. By the time he got home it was raining cats and dogs with the wind blowing hard. He stabled his horse and tended to him and at the house he told Peggy of the stolen cattle.

"Why would anyone steal our cattle?"

"Those cows and bulls are pure bred black angus. Those one thousand and twenty five animals will bring as much money as five thousand longhorns. I don't know exactly when they were rustled. What tracks I saw at the gate appeared to be two days old. These cattle are not used to be driven hard like a bunch of longhorns. If this rain hadn't come along it would be easy to trail them but now the tracks will be washed away. I'll start as soon as it's light enough to see the ground. I will be gone for however long it takes me to find them."

Carlen packed his gear and as he was cleaning his rifle and pistol Peggy said, "Carlen, I thought you were going to stop being a lawman. I am afraid for you to go off by yourself trying to catch whoever stole our cattle."

"Peggy, I don't like what I have to do either, but they are our cattle and it is my responsibility to get them back and if I don't the people here will think me a coward. I'm sure that Bill will go and the two of us can handle this without bloodshed. "

Early the next morning Carlen tied his big dun to the tie rail in front of the café and had a chair at the table always used by Farris. He knew that Sheriff Bill Rose would be the first one to arrive. Betsy placed a cup of coffee before him and asked how he was. "I'm fine, Betsy, I just have a little business to tend to and I want to see Bill this morning. All of us at the ranch really enjoyed the celebration. I think it was the best one I've had the pleasure to attend."

"We all enjoyed it. I hope that we can repeat this kind of show next year."

Bill entered and seated himself across the table from Carlen. They chatted while their breakfast was cooking. Carlen didn't want anyone else to know about the cattle being rustled just yet. After breakfast and the last cup of coffee was finished the two retired to the jail and Bill relieved the night deputy.

"Bill, I just had all of my cattle rustled while we all attended the celebration here in town. I rode out to check on them as soon as we got home yesterday afternoon. The road gate was open and was full of tracks. I found a left front shoe of a toed in foot with a single caulk on the inside part of the shoe. It started raining a heavy down pour before I could begin to try to track them. I had just as soon not let the word out yet as someone might just slip up and ask if I had found them yet."

"Carlen, those are high priced cattle and they will be hard to sell branded as they are. I nearly bet that some crooked rancher within two hundred miles of here stole them to breed up his own stock. Let me get rigged up and I'll meet you at your place and we will start looking for their tracks when the rain stops."

"Ok, Bill, I need to stop at Farris's store and purchase a ground tarp and a new slicker. Is there anything I can pickup for you?"

"Just make sure that we have plenty of shells for our rifles and pistols."

Carlen looped the dun's reins around the tie rack in front of the store and listened to the familiar tinkle of the bell as he entered. Kelly Cleveland was behind the counter filling the rack that held smoking tobacco. "Good morning, Carlen, Farris is in the office doing some book work. Is there something I can help you with?"

"Yes, I need a new slicker and a good ground tarp along with some rifle and pistol shells. Give me two boxes of forty fives and two boxes of thirty thirties and two of forty five seventies. I know where the tarps and slickers are and I'll get them while you get the shells."

"You must be going to hunt bear as many shells as you are buying."

"Not hardly. Most of these are what someone else asked me to pickup for them."

Kelly figured up the bill and Carlen paid him. He told him to tell Farris hello for him as he was in a hurry to meet a fellow. Kelly said he would and for him to tell Peggy hello for them.

When Carlen reached the ranch he stopped by and explained to Pete what had happened and that he and Bill Rose were going after the rustlers. "Pete, I would appreciate it if you would keep this under your hat until we get the cattle back. It might be possible that someone who was helping the rustler might just pop off and ask if we found our cattle."

"I understand, Carlen, and I won't tell anyone anything. If you want me to I would be happy to go along with you two."

"Pete, I appreciate your offer but I need you to stay here and give Peggy all of the help you can. She thinks that something bad might happen to me. You can be her source of faith that everything will turn out alright."

At the house they were living in until their home was finished, Carlen explained to his wife that he and Bill would more than likely be gone for at least a couple of weeks. "Peggy, you just don't worry about me. I'm just not going to let these rustlers take away our livelihood. Bill is going with me and I've told him and Pete not to say a word about this. Someone who is in with the rustlers might just ask if we have found any of our stolen stock."

It wasn't but just a few minutes until Bill arrived. Carlen kissed Peggy goodbye and he and Bill rode to the place where Carlen had seen the tracks.

Tracks would be washed out but cattle and horse droppings would usually remain if the rain didn't dissolve all of it. The most logical direction of travel would be on the road or through open meadows. "Carlen, what day would you think the rustlers hit your herd?"

"It would have had to of been late the evening of the third or early on the fourth. I can't think of anyone who even knew that there were any cattle on the place. Pete had never used the land prior to me buying it. The carpenters building our new home had to have seen or heard cattle but I can't think of anyone else who has been on the place."

"Well, it will take a week for them to drive the herd to Durango if they intend to ship or sell them there. I personally think that someone intends to use them to their own advantage in improving their own cattle. I think we should try riding in a half circle from east to north and then west. I don't think they will try to move that many cattle south over the open country."

"I agree with you, Bill. I don't know this country well enough so you just take the lead and let's get going. I don't think we will find many tracks until we ride to where the rain started. It moved southeast when it hit and the cloud was in the northwest."

"Let's follow the trail that we took those first two outlaws to Mancos on. That trail runs in a northwest to southeast direction."

They rode for four hours without finding any sign. Bill all of a sudden turned south and said, "Carlen, I think we should try the road that leads to Grady Holmes's ranch. I just have a hunch that we will find the tracks there."

By the time the two riders reached the road they had run out of the area that the rain had soaked. Bill was right; at least cattle had been driven down this road headed west. Carlen searched the road bed and found the toed in print that was at the gate. "Bill, this is the same horse shoe print that I found at my place before the rain came. We are on the right trail now. Thanks to you for thinking that they might use this road."

"It was really just a guess, Carlen. These guys know this country pretty well too. Not far from where we left the trail we were on, it becomes too rough and narrow to drive this many cattle on. I doubt if they will stay on this road. Somewhere up ahead I think they will turn back north and try to stay in the timber and lose their tracks again. I know that there is not a creek strong enough to hide their tracks in so they must be trying to find another trail or road to make better time on. There are some shipping pens in Dolores. I don't think they would take them there. There are too many people around there that knows Pete and his cattle. They are still carrying his brand, aren't they?"

"Thank goodness yes. I didn't want to vent the brand that Pete had on them. I want to put my brand on their offspring. I thought that Pete would like it better if I did it that way."

Bill was right about them leaving the road to go north. They ran the cattle into a sandy wash on the north side of the road. If the rain had reached this area the tracks would have been washed out. The two followed the wash until the banks started becoming steep. The rustlers had driven the cattle out of the wash on the east side and the trail continued on in a northerly direction. The sun was slipping behind the mountains and Bill told Carlen that there was a seep just ahead and they could spend the night there and take the trail again as soon as it was light enough to see.

Bill gathered up firewood and had coffee boiling by the time Carlen had unsaddled and hobbled their mounts. "You know, Bill, that we are headed directly toward Mancos. The only thing that is between us and Bud Wheeler's store is Mesa Verde."

"Yes, I just wished that I knew which direction they will go when they get close to the cliffs. If I did know we could cut across and gain a day on them."

"Well, Bill, they will have to go east or west to get around the mesa. I would bet that they will turn west. If they go east some of the ranchers in that area are bound to see Pete's brand on the cattle and we would get word of it.

"If they stay on the east side they could turn west again as soon as they cleared the mesa. They could drive the herd due west after dark and could not be seen by the people in Mancos. Another night of driving would take them past Cortez and they would have clear sailing all the way across Utah Territory."

Carlen asked, "Bill, is there any way we could get on top of Mesa Verde to where we could see the country and maybe see their dust?"

"There are a couple of trails going up on this south side but it is hard on a horse. We could lead them if you feel like a two hour climb in your boots. Then there is a straight trail leading to Mancos. We can see for miles on top. I think you have a good idea, Carlen. We can gain almost a day and pick up a few supplies at the Wheeler store."

After a quick breakfast, washed down with hot coffee, they saddled up and rode straight for the trail to the top of Mesa Verde.

Bill was right about the trail being hard on man and beast alike. They were on the flat top of the mesa an hour before noon. They let their horses blow while they gave their feet a rub down. The view was something to behold as you could see for miles in any direction. Carlen pointed to the northeast and said, "Bill, I believe that the moving mass of black is what we are looking for."

The herd was being driven by six riders and was being turned to the west to follow a trail at the base of the mesa. The closest village was Mancos and they would bed down the herd before they got within sight of it. "Carlen, the trail down is a little father on west and we can reach Wheeler's place without being seen as the trail goes down a wash. We can be at the store in three hours. That will give us time enough to see if we can find a couple of men or more to help us arrest these rustlers. I'm sure Bud Wheeler knows some lawman or a few cowboys who would gladly lend us a hand."

Going down was a whole lot easier than going up. It might have been harder on their horses but it was a lot better on the riders.

Bud Wheeler greeted them with a hand shake and told them to take a chair and he would have the coffee on the table in a few minutes as Mother Wheeler just put on a fresh pot.

Carlen asked, "Bud, do you reckon that your good wife has a little something to stuff down two hungry cowboys?"

"If she doesn't she will have by the time you are on your second cup. What brings you two over here anyway?"

Carlen told him of the stolen cattle and asked if he might know of a lawman or someone who they might get to help them round up the rustlers and then the cattle.

"We don't have an officer of the law here in Mancos yet but I know some Ex-Texas Rangers and some retired U.S. Marshals who would be glad to give you a hand. They haven't had any excitement here in a few years. I think you boys would fit right in with them. I'll send my stable hand over to the D bar K ranch and we'll see how many men they can spare to help you two."

While the rider was headed to the ranch Carlen and Bill enjoyed Mother Wheeler's home cooking.

In about three hours the stable man returned bringing two riders with him. One was a tall lanky man around forty years of age with a little gray showing in his sideburns. The other was a few years younger and they both looked like they had just come off of the range. The tall one stuck out his hand and said in a Texas drawl, "Fellers, I'm Clint Caraday and this gent is Roy Coleman. We were the only two around when Bud's man told us you all needed a little help."

Carlen introduced Bill and himself and asked them to have a cup of coffee while he explained the situation.

Clint spoke, "I know that this bunch of rustlers is headed for the canyons over in Utah. It seems like the folks over there just can't get enough of these Black Angus cattle. We've had our share of them trying to steal some of ours ever since I've been here. Well, since you say there are only six of them I don't see any problem with us four taking back what's yours. How about we ride out there tonight and catch them early in the morning before they get their eyes opened good? Since Roy and I haven't had any lunch yet we might as well tank up on some of the best home cooking in the country."

Clint and Roy told them that Judge Hayes spoke highly of them for what they had done for the folks in San Juan County. Clint told them that he enjoyed everything about being a Texas Ranger except the food and the pay. "I met my best friend while I was stationed with him. When he left the Rangers and came up here, I joined him the first chance I got. Roy was already here when Dan came up, but we're all from Texas. Our old Ranger Captain moved up when he retired and when Marshal Moss Milburn retired he moved in over at the ranch too. You fellers need to come over and meet the rest of us when you get a chance."

The July sun finally hid itself beyond Sleeping Ute Mountain and the four men saddled up and checked their weapons and rode into the darkening night. As they rode two abreast Clint told Carlen that there was usually some big rancher over in Utah that hires these rustlers to steal the cattle, then he forges a bill of sale and the rustlers disappear. "We caught one a few years back that was a first class robber baron. Moss along with Roy and a couple more marshals caught him and five of his henchmen over in a little stage stop called Blanding. They had a big shoot out and killed three of them and wound up getting the big boss and one of the other two hung. One, the judge gave a light sentence to for locating a bunch of homesteads that big boss had stolen and people he had murdered. This feller was a man with no heart or feelings about anyone or anything. He even killed a few women folks. Moss made a believer out of him before they got him to the jail in Durango."

They could see the smoldering camp fire from the top of the rise where they watched four of them bed down as two were riding night hawk duty on the cattle. At midnight the two riders were relieved and two more took their place. At three o'clock the last two sleepers took the last shift. Clint noticed that one of these was an awful small man or just a young boy.

Clint said, "Fellers, I will go around and take care of these two night herders and you all just wait here 'til I get back."

By four o'clock Clint was back and told them that he had the two bound and gagged and that one of them was a boy about twelve years old. "The other, the boy told me, was the camp cook. He said that he was an orphan and he was working for room and board. The cook is as old as a man can get before dying of old age. Neither one of them had a gun of any kind on them or in their saddle bags nor was there a rifle scabbard on either horse. I think that we have evened the odds and before these sleepers wake up we need to form a half circle around them and give them a chance to surrender or to die right here."

Clint told them that since Roy was a married man with a beautiful little daughter that he should find some protection in case there was a gun fight. They agreed and started looking for the best spot to shoot from in case these rustlers didn't want to give up without a fight.

The cattle that were bedded down began to stir and start looking for something to graze on. One of the rustlers sat up in his blankets and called for the cook to come in and start some breakfast. Bill told him to raise his hands above his head and stand up. Instead the man dropped on his stomach and pulled a pistol from under the covers. Bill shot him just as he squeezed the trigger of his weapon. The bullet hit the ground a foot in front of Bill as he shot again when the outlaw raised his pistol for another try. He never made it.

Shots were coming from the other three rustlers as they tried and failed to hit their adversaries. The cattle moved farther away from the camp but never broke into a stampede. When the smoke cleared there were four dead men someone had to bury.

Carlen found the old cook and the boy, untied them and brought them back to camp. The cook Said, "Well, I guess that I might as well cook us up a good breakfast, that's what I was hired to do."

While the man built up the fire and was cooking the others searched the four dead men then rolled them in their blankets and placed them in a wash and after caving the banks on them covered the earth with the abundance of rocks in the area. The boy didn't say a word. He just helped cover the bodies, always looking at the ground. Carlen told the youngster to walk over to the creek and wash up and get ready for breakfast. The boy just turned and walked to the creek. Roy said, "That little boy is going to have a hard time overcoming what we did here this morning. I went through it my first time as a young man and it took me a few years to block it from my mind."

When the cook called them to breakfast Carlen told the youngster to grab a plate and get after it. The boy took a tin plate and cup and let the old cook place a couple of flapjacks on it and pour him a cup of coffee. Carlen passed him the syrup bottle and watched him pour the thick molasses over the cakes; after a second or two hunger got the best of the little fellow and he put those away and asked if he could have another. The old cook smiled and placed two more on his plate.

After the meal was finished Clint asked, "Do you two fellows think you can drive this herd back by yourselves? Roy and I both have to get back to our work or we would give you a hand with them. We would like to take Cookie back with us and let him tell Judge Hayes who the big shot of this operation is."

Bill asked, "What if Cookie doesn't want to go back?"

"Well, if that's the way he feels about it I guess we could just put him over there with the people he has been associating with."

"Fellers, I never seen any of these men or this boy here until I was hired on to be a cook for a small herd of cattle. The man who hired me is some kind of a preacher or school teacher over in Utah. I'll be more than glad to tell your judge all I know about this mess. I never had any idea that we were stealing these cattle. The trail boss that you boys shot knew exactly where he was going and he just told us to run them out and get them headed for Utah. You can ask the boy if I ain't telling you the truth."

Carlen looked at the boy as he was swigging down the last of his coffee. "Young man, can you give us your name and where your home is?"

"Yes, Sir, my name is Jimmy Green and I don't have a home any more. My daddy got killed when a horse reared over backwards and the saddle horn crushed his heart. My mother had to leave me at an orphans home while she worked but she took bad sick and died from what the doctor said was pneumonia. I was eight years old then and I stayed in the orphanage until I was ten then I ran away. I did any kind of a Job that I could do and this man that wanted the cattle drove over to his ranch gave me five dollars if I would help. I was out of work and real hungry so I took the job. I don't know any of the men that you shot and the only one that showed me any kindness was the cook."

"Well, what if I paid you ten dollars to help Bill and me drive these cattle back to where they came from?"

"I sure would appreciate it. I still have the five dollars that the man in Utah paid me."

"Well, Jimmy, pick you out one of these horses and get a good saddle and we will get started home." Bill and Carlen shook hands with Clint and Roy and told them how much they appreciated their help.

Clint said, "You fellers make it a point to come up to see us when you have a chance. Just stop in at Bud Wheelers and he can tell you where we live. It was really a good feeling to get to work with a couple of Texans again."

As they rode off Clint said to Roy, "That boy back there sure makes me think of Buttons when we first saw him."

Roy said, "Clint, you must have been reading my mind, I was thinking the same thing."

The cook shook hands with them and told them to take care of the boy. Carlen assured him they would and for him to tell Judge Hayes about the man in Utah.

There were two pack horses and eight saddle horses left after Cookie saddled one up and followed Clint and Roy. Jimmy got the small short coupled bay that he had been riding and picked out a decent saddle and threw his old one in the wash. Carlen and Bill saddled up three of the others and tied the stirrups together to keep them from flapping and scaring the horse.

There wasn't really too much to driving these cattle as they were used to trailing by now and they weren't prone to run or stampede. Bill took the point with the pack horses and the others trailing behind him. Carlen and Jimmy were working the drag. It was an eight or ten mile day at the best. They never crowded the cattle as a cow has a certain walking speed and you're better off not to try to hurry them up. Eight days later they had the herd back where they started from.

Peggy was glad to see her husband as was Pete Johnson. Bill spent the night and with a good bath and shave felt like a new man. Carlen told Jimmy to take a bath and be ready for supper.

Pete had the four of them at his big house for supper. Carlen filled him in about Jimmy and Bill told him of the job of getting the stock back. Neither he nor Carlen either one mentioned the demise of the four rustlers. When Pete asked, they just told him that Clint Caraday and Roy Coleman took care of them. They were going to see Judge Hayes because one of them wanted to spill the beans about the man that hired them to do it.

Early the next morning as soon as breakfast was over Bill told them bye and headed back to his job as Sheriff of San Juan County.

Carlen rolled out the new buggy and hooked up the pair of gray geldings and with Peggy, Pete and Jimmy aboard took his time on the trip to town.

The first stop was at the big store of Farris Baker. Kelly shook their hands and Farris was happy to see them. Peggy said, "Kelly, we have just hired us a new cowboy and he lost his valise somewhere and we need to outfit him with a complete new wardrobe from the ground up and make sure that he has plenty of changes. I'll go with you two and give you my approval or rejection."

While Peggy picked out the wearing apparel of a cowboy for Jimmy Green, Farris told Carlen that Curtiss needed to see him. "He told me if you didn't come in today to town that he was coming out to the ranch tonight. It must be something important because the messenger from Judge Hayes was in here this morning and had to wait until Curtiss got to his office."

Carlen told Peggy that he was going to see Curtiss and would be back in a few minutes.

Curtiss was at his desk buried in paper work when Carlen walked into his office. He arose from behind his desk and after a handshake with his brother-in-law asked him to pull up a chair.

"Carlen, I received an urgent notice from Judge Hayes early this morning. He has instructed me to swear you and Bill in as U.S. Marshals. Evidently you and Bill had a run in with some rustlers and the one your friend Clint brought in to his office has given him all of the information that he needs to put the big boss away for a long time. He has instructed me to have you and Bill report to Bud Wheeler in Mancos for a packet with names, maps and other information that you will need to arrest this man and bring him to Durango for trial. The judge is sending this packet on the train and you are given the power to swear in as many men as you need. There will be your power of attorney and extra badges in the packet."

"Bill and I just got home last night; I just hope that I'm not taking anything away from the town or county by asking Bill to go with me."

"Not at all, Carlen, this matter has precedence over everything else."

"Well, Curtiss, I reckon I'd better get a hold of Bill and tell your sister that I'll be gone again for a few days. I know that she is going to be a little upset but it's a job that's got to be done."

Peggy wasn't really very happy about the matter but she understood. Since Jimmy Green had been added to the payroll she told Carlen that she would take care of him and let him be her body guard. Bill just grinned and said I'll get my gear and meet you at the ranch.

Chapter Eighteen

Carlen filled Pete in on what was happening on the way back to the ranch. "Bill and I both told Judge Hayes that we would do our duty anytime he needed us. I know that he doesn't have another lawman west or south of Durango. I just hope that this part of the country runs out of outlaws pretty quick. I swore to Peggy that I was just going to be a cowboy after we cleaned up the mess in San Juan. I hope she doesn't think that Bill and I are making a habit of this."

Peggy and Jimmy were in the back seat of the buggy and she spoke up, "Carlen, I was there when you and Bill told the judge you would render your help as it was needed. I don't like for you to have to do this but I'm proud of you for doing it. These people that you two are going after are guilty of stealing our livelihood. Just think of all of the other people that have been hurt. I believe when the judge gets through with the punishment it will be a lesson to others who are intending to follow in these types of crimes."

Carlen had his gear packed on a pack horse and had enough for the needs of both men for a week. Since he had used his big dun horse on the last trip he had saddled the bay and was ready to leave as soon as Bill arrived.

He kissed Peggy goodbye and told Jimmy to take good care of things until he got back. Pete had taken the boy under his wing like an old mother hen would do a baby chick. The boy would be loved and well taken care of. The crew treated him as if he was already one of them. Jimmy Green had reasons to have a smile on his face.

The two marshals took the same trail as before and Carlen told Bill that he could remember his way in the dark. Three hard days of riding brought them to Wheeler's store at twilight. Mother Wheelers cooking never tasted better and they would have a roof over their heads in Bud's cabin tonight. The packet had been there for the last three days and Bud knew that it was something important coming from Judge Hayes. Carlen and Bill read the letter and looked at the map that was drawn by the cook who Clint had taken to Durango.

Bud told them that he had never heard of Simon Goodlove which was the man the warrant was made out for. The map was well drawn and showed the Goodlove ranch about twenty miles west of Cortez and was bisected by McElmo Creek. The creek turned into being a fair sized canyon the farther west it went. The letter explained that there were usually three hands at the ranch the few days that the cook was there. His description of Goodlove showed him to be a man about thirty years old and was red headed. He wore his pistol tied down low on his right hip and also carried a smaller pistol in a shoulder holster. He was described as being hot tempered and would fight at the drop of a hat. There was never a woman or any children around for the three days the cook was there. One of the three men was doing the cooking until he was hired for the trail drive. None of the three at the ranch went with the other four rustlers.

Carlen said, "Well, Bill, let's get a good night's rest and we'll ride over to the Goodlove ranch tomorrow and see if we can persuade the man to come peaceful. If he doesn't want to I guess we will just have to bring him in one way or another."

They told the Wheelers that they would see them in the morning for breakfast and would like for Bud to stable their pack horse until they returned.

Noon found them at a livery stable in Cortez where they unsaddled their mounts to give them a quart of oats and water. The hostler directed them to a café where they had lunch and enjoyed a second cup of coffee. Bill asked, "Carlen, how do you think we should handle this situation with four men?"

"Bill, all I know is that we'll just have to see what's there and how the redhead will react when I hand him the arrest warrant. We might have a four to two gun fight, but I sure hope not.

"Maybe I should go in with the warrant by myself and you can position yourself behind some place where you could back me up with your rifle. You can never tell. He may be there alone or just maybe the others want to stay out of the fight if he goes for a weapon."

"Carlen, I don't want you there in front of him by yourself. If one of the others or maybe two of them want to back him up you won't stand much of a chance."

"Well, let's just play it by ear and wait until we scout the place before we ride in."

Back at the livery stable Carlen asked the hostler directions to the Goodlove ranch. The old fellow gave him a frown and asked him if they planned to go to work there. "No, we just have some business with a man by the name of Simon Goodlove."

"I don't know what kind of business you have with him but you had better be careful of how you talk to Simon, sometimes I think he's half cracked. At times he's as wild as a March hare and mean as a loco wolf. He keeps two or three men around him at all times. You had better let him know that you're coming or they might shoot first and talk later."

After they were in the saddle headed down McElmo Creek Bill said, "Well, the hostler doesn't seem to think very much of Mister Goodlove. We had better be ready to shoot if any one of them makes a move toward a weapon."

"We should get there a couple of hours before dark and I don't want to face the sun when we call him out. You stand clear of me, Bill, and watch the others. If one of them makes a move kill him and I'll do the same. Once the shooting starts they won't stop until they are dead. This is the worst part about being an officer of the law, but it just goes with the job."

When they came into view of the ranch they checked their pistols and rifles and made sure that there was a shell in each chamber. The buildings set on a flat area of a rust covered rock. The creek bed had widened out and the entire wash was solid rock. Trees were sparse on the banks above the creek and it didn't look much like cattle country. The two marshals rode up to the tie rail in front of the plank board house and dismounted. Carlen walked up to the porch and called if anyone was home. A short stocky man with a bushy beard stepped out and asked what they wanted. Carlen replied, "We have important business with Simon Goodlove."

"Tell me what kind of business and I'll go get him."

"I'd rather tell Mister Goodlove myself if you don't mind."

Bill was watching each corner of the house while Carlen kept his eyes on the man at the door. Someone in the house called "What's going on out there Shorty?"

"A couple of gents say they have some business with you and they won't tell me what it is. "

"Alright, I'll be out there in a few minutes. You just stay there with them till I get there. I've got to run out to the barn first and check on Clem."

The two marshals knew that he was going to alert the other two of his men. He was back in a few minutes and stepped out on the porch with Shorty. "What can I do for you two gentlemen?" The redhead stood there with his feet apart and an unlighted cigar clenched in his teeth. His coat was open and he held a fake smile on his face.

Carlen was about ten feet from him and was standing on the ground which was a couple of feet lower than the porch. "Mister Goodlove, we have a warrant for your arrest from Judge Hayes in Durango."

"Well, just let me light my cigar and I'll take a look at your warrant." He opened the lapel of his coat with his left hand and reached inside the coat. Carlen then shot him twice as he pulled out a short barrel revolver. The pistol dropped to the porch and Goodlove fell from the porch into the yard. Shorty was not armed and Bill shot one man as he came around the corner of the house with a pistol in his hands. The other one came through the front door and shoved Shorty aside to get a clear shot at Carlen. Bill and Carlen both fired at the man at the same time before he could fire his weapon. Shorty raised his hands and screamed, "Please don't kill me, I'm not armed and I don't know what this is all about."

The two marshals handcuffed Shorty to a post that was holding up the front porch and then searched the three dead men. A search of the house produced evidence of the identity of all three men who were wanted in Arizona for cattle rustling and murder. They could not find any proof of Shorty's past. After they had questioned him and found out that he was a newly hired hand, they had no choice but to release him.

Carlen looked the man straight in the eyes and told him, "We will let you go free if you can tell us who gave Goodlove the information of the cattle he had tried to steal in San Juan County."

"I'll tell you what I know but I never heard any names. There was a feller came by here a couple of months ago and told Simon about the black cattle. He told him that some rancher named Pete Johnson hung his brother a few months back and of the big blow out that the town was having for the Fourth of July. He told Simon that he could easily rustle the cattle and he would go help him."

"What about the young boy that he sent along to help steal the cattle?"

"The poor kid was just a waif that come along and asked for a job. The kid was half starved and Simon had hired an old man to cook for the drive. The old man told Simon that he could use the boy to help with the drive and gather fire wood. He told him that he would give him five dollars out of his own pocket. Simon must have had a little feeling about the kid because he pulled out a five dollar gold piece and gave it to him. I truly believe that was the only time in Simon's life he ever did anything good for another soul."

"Shorty, I don't know what the judge is going to do with whatever property that Simon has but if you want to help the people that he has hurt or robbed you could tell the court about it."

"I ain't been here long enough to know anything that I haven't already told you. If you don't mind I'll bury these three and then saddle my horse and leave the country."

The two marshals shook his hand and told him to stay out of trouble. He guaranteed he would.

It was dark as they dismounted in front of the livery stable in Cortez. The hostler grinned when he greeted them. "Well, I guess you two couldn't find Simon Goodlove could you?"

Bill said, "We found him, but there is no use of anyone else trying to find him. He is in a place no one else should ever want to see."

They got a room at the hotel and after a bath and shave they slept on feather beds for a change. By noon the next day they were at Mother Wheeler's table enjoying her good cooking. They paid up their bill of fare and told the Wheelers goodbye, leading their pack horse headed for San Juan.

Three days later Carlen and Bill arrived at the ranch where they were greeted with a warm welcome. Bill spent the night and left after breakfast to resume his duty as Sheriff of San Juan County and to inform Judge Hayes of their mission. Carlen, Peggy and Jimmy stayed in the kitchen and lingered over another cup of coffee with Pete. Man it sure was good to be home again.

The End

Alex Alexander is a sixth generation Texan having spent the majority of his life on a ranch in central Texas that boasts the proximity of the Old Chisholm Trail. Millions of Longhorn cattle were herded up the trail bound for railroad shipping pens in Kansas and Missouri. The area is rich with history and legend having both fictional and factual stories being passed down from generation to generation. Alex is surrounded by his multitude of children, grand-children and great-grandchildren who never miss an opportunity to listen to Papa weave his magical tales of cowboys and Indians from long ago. A rancher never really retires, so he now spends his time sharing his family tales to all.

Other books by Alex Alexander

Once A Ranger Always A Ranger

A Time In Texas

Sandstone

Finders Keepers

Alex Alexander

Made in the USA
Columbia, SC
28 September 2017